# Universal Santa

Second Paperback Edition

Copyright © 2014 by k.m. Starr
Cover Design by Kristi Carr
Published by k.m. Starr
Illustrations by k.m. Starr

ISBN: 978-0-9911408-1-7

# Universal Santa

k.m. Starr

## Acknowledgements

My thanks go to…

all who stood by me and encouraged me
when I hit a virtual brick wall;

*

my boss, who put up with impromptu
vacation days when the words were bub-
bling out like a shaken bottle of champagne;

*

Kristina for keeping me grounded and helping with the style, layout and graphics –
I value your opinion;

*

my editors – without whom, this book
would still be unfinished (you know who
you are)

*

my dad, because he believed in me and
pushed me along to actually get this
published.

*Thanks, Dad!*

*Dedication*

This book is dedicated to my mother, who gave me an idea and let me run with it.

*Thanks, Mom, you are my rock!*

# Table of Contents

*The Universe* .................................................................................. viii
Prologue............................................................................................ix
Flight to Earth ............................................................................... 1
*Beeb's First Report* ...................................................................... 17
Arriving on Earth .......................................................................... 21
*Communication (Coms) Unit* ................................................... 36
Tony.................................................................................................. 37
Seeking Santa ................................................................................. 47
*Profile – Frankle* .......................................................................... 62
*Beeb's Second Report* ................................................................. 63
*Profile – Reyclebin*....................................................................... 66
North Pole ....................................................................................... 67
*Profile –Frinkle*............................................................................. 76
Seattle............................................................................................... 77
Traveling South ............................................................................. 87
*Profile – Limdon*........................................................................... 92
*Beeb's Third Report*..................................................................... 93
Hollywood, CA............................................................................... 97
*Profile – Morach*......................................................................... 106
Morach's Movie ........................................................................... 107
*Profile – Beeb*.............................................................................. 120
*Beeb's Fourth Report*................................................................. 121
*Profile – Pumbint*....................................................................... 124
Limdon and Pumbint's Secret ................................................... 125
*Profile – Vedagy*......................................................................... 138
Uruguay......................................................................................... 139
*Profile – Pader*............................................................................ 156
Africa.............................................................................................. 157
*Profile – Tony*.............................................................................. 176
*Beeb's Fifth Report* .................................................................... 177
*Profile – Clombic*........................................................................ 180
Ethiopia......................................................................................... 181
Paris................................................................................................ 201
*Profile – Portamer* ..................................................................... 210
Meeting Santa .............................................................................. 211
*Profile – Santa*............................................................................ 218
Christmas....................................................................................... 219

*Profile – Presents* ................................................................228
Gifts ........................................................................................229
*Profile –Truth Glasses* ........................................................236
*Beeb's Sixth Report* ..............................................................237
*Galactic-Day to Earth-Hours Conversion Table* ...................240
Epilogue ................................................................................241
About the Author ................................................................244

# The Universe

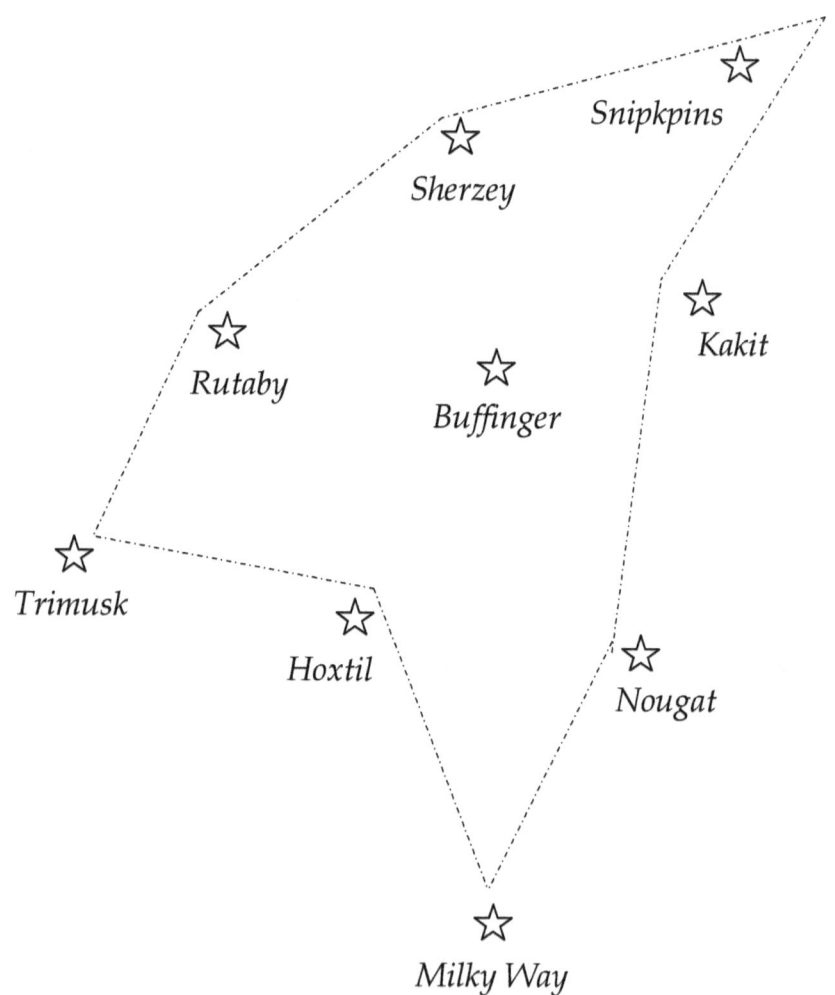

# Prologue

"The studies have shown the negative waves are over-whelming and there is no happiness among the humans of Earth. We will destroy…"

"But, Sir," cried Morach, interrupting the oration of their leader, Reyclebin. "I believe the data is incomplete."

"What do you mean, Morach? Your department submitted its findings ahead of schedule and you are saying it is incomplete?" Reyclebin's voice held both surprise and indignation at this new bit of information. Though he was a gentle soul by nature, he didn't like being made a fool of; and having partial information for such a monumental decision was not to his liking – it was down-right embarrassing.

"Exactly, Sir. The report was submitted without my approval…"

"Way to go, one eye!" yelled someone

from the observation gallery. The meeting room housed a large, round, solid cherry-wood table capable of seating up to twenty-four council members and guests. The table could be lowered into the floor during social events. It also had a stage – complete with a sound system for the larger functions. A small seating area for guest speakers and galactic dignitaries was at the rear of the room.

The second level of the arena housed a balcony-style observation gallery. It over-looked the meeting room on three sides and held several smaller meeting rooms on the fourth. The gallery had stadium seating capable of holding two-hundred bodies. It was bordered by a three-foot banister and a protective sheet of shatterproof glass that allowed spectators to walk to their seats and watch the proceedings without fear of falling. Audio speakers were positioned in such a way that everyone could hear the proceedings no matter where they were seated. Today, all the seats were filled.

"That will be enough!" exclaimed Reyclebin as he stood and addressed the gallery. His mood was already on edge and he didn't have patience for hecklers interrupting his meeting. "There will be no further outbursts from the gallery or I will close off this meeting." All council meetings were open to the general public, but the president of the council had the power to close the meeting. He need only press a button to engage the sight-and-sound-proof curtain across the front of the observation area – which also disengaged the speakers.

"Please continue, Morach – without interruption," Reyclebin said pointedly as he looked at the gallery with silent admonition and resumed his seat.

"Thank you, Sir. As you know, our data was gathered using Earth's satellite signals; but I don't believe we should base the end of a planet on only one type of information. My assistant misunderstood me when I commented that we had all the information we were going to get from those signals. He took that to mean our study was complete; whereas, I believe we need further study from another angle."

"What other angle do you suggest?" one of the council members asked.

Taking a deep breath, Morach closed his eye to gather his courage then opened it and spoke without further hesitation. "I think we should get a closer look before we destroy the humans. I suggest we go to Earth for further study." The room erupted into dead silence as everyone held their breath and looked to Reyclebin for direction.

"Very well, Morach, we will put it to a vote. All those in favor of sending a committee to study the humans before making a final decision on the fate of Earth, press your indicators." The lights for seven of the nine Galactic Council members lit up. "Those opposed?" The two remaining members pressed their indicators.

"Let the record show the results. We will visit Earth to gather the final data before deciding its fate. I suggest we send a representative from each galaxy to Earth for five days – that is five Earth weeks – plus one day for travel each direction. We will reconvene in eight galactic days and the committee will present any evidence it finds to determine the fate of Earth.

"I charge each council member to choose one Being from his or her galaxy to be on the committee. We will meet here tonight when the galaxies are in alignment." Seeing the eagerness of the other members, Reyclebin adjourned the meeting.

"Rey, I know what you are thinking." Falcyn, who had the privilege of sitting in the dignitary seats along with the other spouses, pulled her husband aside while the others left the room. "You simply cannot go to Earth. You are the President of the Universal Council of Galaxies. What if something were to happen to you? What would I do without you? What would the Council do?"

Falcyn and Reyclebin met when they were children and married after Reyclebin finished his education. They have been married for forty years but have been unsuccessful in having any children of their own. Reyclebin was all the family Falcyn had left and she didn't want to lose him any time soon.

"Now, now, Falcyn," Reyclebin pulled her into a loose embrace. "You know as well as I that this voyage will need an experienced leader to manage the team."

"But..."

"No buts. I will be fine and I promise I will return with the entire committee. Besides, Vice-President Orab will step up if something unforeseen should happen."

"That just proves my point," she reasoned. "We have no idea what will happen." Resigned to his decision, Falcyn held further protests – though not without misgivings. She knew she wouldn't win this argument and didn't want to put any additional stress on her husband before a potentially dangerous mission. Better that he had her support than her fears and worries.

* * * * *

Reyclebin held private audiences with each of the Council members and their chosen representatives for final approval. Only one was rejected for his deceptive motives. He planned to sabotage the ship to strand them on Earth. In so doing, they would be unable to return and the Council would destroy Earth – proving to his followers that anything is possible. Fortunately, the Council member had an alternative choice that was approved. The representatives were chosen and the committee to Search for Happiness and Assess the Destiny of Earth (S.H.A.D.E.) was born.

## one

## Flight to Earth

"We have just entered the Milky Way Galaxy," Captain Pader announced. Although he had been running a shuttle between galaxies for many years, Pader had never been to Earth and regarded this as an adventure to add to his list of accomplishments upon his return.

"My fellow committee members," Reyclebin called the room to attention. "Most of you have explored the ship by now and found your sleeping quarters – one for the three girls and two for the five boys. Pader and I have our own rooms. Your belongings have been placed in your rooms. Clombic, your area has a suspended rod in lieu of a standard bed, as requested."

Clombic could have been offended by being called a *girl* rather than a *woman*, but she understood that the generic term used throughout the galaxies for females was *girls,* while *boys* was generic for males – regardless of age.

"Thank you, Sir." Clombic came from a race that sleeps wrapped around a bar rather than lying prone on a mattress. This makes it convenient to hide in a forest while on reconnaissance. She can wrap her three long legs around a tree limb and survey her surroundings. Her single eye revolves around her head like a beacon – allowing her to see in any direction. To sleep, she wraps her legs around the limb and leans against the tree trunk – or wall if she is inside.

"I've spoken with each of you individually regarding your role in this mission, but now it is time to officially meet each other. I will begin:

"As you know, my name is Reyclebin and I am the President of the Universal Council of Galaxies. As such, I have appointed myself Chairman of the committee to Search for Happiness and Assess the Destiny of Earth. For purposes of this mission, you are to call me Rey; not Sir, Reyclebin, Mr. President, or Chairman. It will be much simpler." He gave a questioning look and everyone nodded their understanding. "I was born on the planet Bolcus in the Buffinger Galaxy. I bring my 40 years of leadership experience to this mission and look forward to working with all of you on this very important voyage."

The room erupted with cheers and applause as he sat down. After a moment, Reyclebin nodded at Vedagy sitting to his left – giving her the signal to proceed. As she stood, the applause quieted.

"My name is Vedagy, but my friends call me Veda. I hail from planet Noslaw of the Rutaby Galaxy. I am well-versed in the herb properties of many galaxies and can make a meal – or a poultice for any illness that may arise – with whatever herbs and plants are available. In other words, I am a cook and a healer." Giggles circled the table as she sat and the next member stood.

"I am Pumbint which shortens to Punt. I represent Edabel in the Nougat Galaxy. I am an inventor of electronic devices and have some equipment that will help us communicate on Earth." Looking to Reyclebin for the okay to reveal the details, he continued. "Limmy will be giving each of you a translating device that will allow communications with anyone. The device is programmed for all of the dialects of every language spoken on Earth for the past 800 years. Regardless who you speak with, they will understand you in their own language and you will understand them. In addition, I can make repairs to our ship as well as operate and repair any electronics we may encounter on Earth."

"Wow, Punt, that's awesome! I wish I had that kind of skill." Awestruck, Frinkle was motioned to continue with his introduction. "Right. So, I'm Frinkle from Pluto in the Milky Way Galaxy. Yup, Earth is in my galaxy," he said with a Cheshire cat's grin. "As a matter of fact, the reason I'm here is that my cousin, Frankle, immigrated to Earth a few years ago and works for a millionaire who has properties all over the world – which is what the humans call Earth. My cousin can get us shelter at hotels in places we may visit." Feeling proud of himself, Frinkle took his seat.

"I am Portamer," began the next in the circle. "You may call me Portamer. I was born on the planet Dunkis in the galaxy of Trimusk. We of Dunkis are great skeptics. My role is to keep everyone from becoming awestruck," he emphasized this statement with a stern look at

Frinkle who noticeably sunk lower into his chair but still sported a  silly grin. "I am a professor of anthropology and have studied the lifestyles of humans.  I am not easily amused and do not expect to find happiness on Earth."

"My given name is Limdon, but everyone calls me Limmy.  I was born on Conog in the Hoxtil Galaxy – between the Trimusk and Nougat galaxies.  I am trained in the art of crystal energy.  Punt and I combined our devices into one for convenience and practicality.  I will be giving each of you a crystal attached to either a choker band or a wrist band.  These will need to be worn at all times on Earth.  These crystals will give you the appearance of humans to anyone you meet. No one will be able to tell that you are not from the human race.  Frinkle may be able to go without one as he depicts some of the human forms, but the rest of us will not blend in without these crystals.

"The crystals also act as locators if we happen to get separated.  The energy conducted through crystals can also provide power for our needs.  This ship, for example, is powered by panels lined with crystals to harness the energy from the suns and, with Punt's alterations, will transform and become our transportation on Earth." Everyone at the table, except Portamer, was focused on the crystal Limdon was holding. As she put it on, she was seemingly altered into a human body. A collective, "Ahhh" spread around the room. "Punt and I will speak with you in smaller groups to explain what each crystal controls and how to use the coms unit – that's what we are calling the communication device. Thank you."

"Morach, or Mark, here. I led the research party that gathered the information from the Earth's satellites. The data showed a lot of negativity, but something tells me it isn't indicative of the nature of humans. I will find out what was transmitted on those satellites when we get to Earth." He started to sit then added, "Oh, yes, I am from Tivar in the Kakit Galaxy. Thank you."

"Hi. I'm Beeb from Sniggins in the Snipkpins Galaxy. I won the lottery from my galaxy and was awarded the honor of joining this mission. I like to think I can read minds, too, but it hasn't been tested. I'll sit down now."

"Beeb will also be our record keeper," Reyclebin interjected. "He will create daily reports – that's weekly on Earth – to document our progress. Thank you, Beeb."

"Don't worry Beeb, honey, you will be just fine," stated the last member of the committee in her southern drawl. "I am Cloe, short for Clombic, born on planet Shascan in the Sherzey Galaxy. I am along to add an additional female perspective. We wouldn't want anyone sayin' Earth was destroyed because of a biased male view now, would we?" With a half-smile, she continued. "Seriously, I have weapons trainin' if the need should arise. We can all hope it doesn't; but the reality is that if the negativity found in the original data is correct, we may need to protect ourselves. I have trainin' in all manner of weaponry including fire arms, knives, and physical combat. I am also considered a sharp-shooter."

It was difficult to imagine Clombic doing hand-to-hand combat; however, she had the advantage of 360 degree vision and a body that rotated in three independent sections: head; torso, including her three arms; and her lower body. Perhaps that was what made her effective – nobody would believe she could succeed.

"Thank you all. You each have a role and your galaxies did well with their choices. I would also like to introduce Pader, our captain for this endeavor." Pader put the ship on auto-pilot for a few minutes so he could be introduced. They still had a couple of hours to go until they landed.

"Hi, everyone."

"Hi, Pader," they answered in return.

"Pader has been the exclusive shuttle driver for the Galactic Council for the past ten years and has been a long-time family friend. As we wanted to keep our number small to reduce our presence on Earth, Pader is the sole pilot. We may ask that some of you assist from time to time to give him some rest when necessary. Hopefully, we will not be traveling long periods of time as we need to interact and observe the humans as much as possible – but we do have a long week ahead of us.

"Do you have any questions so far?" Reyclebin asked. "I have a few more announcements before we prepare to land." He pulled out several large packages from the cabinet at the front of the room. "During your interview sessions, each of you was asked what colors best define you and why. Using that information, I commissioned special suits tailored to each person in his (or her) described colors. Collectively, we shall look like the alleged rainbow." Everyone snickered at his analogy.

"Cloe, would you assist me?" Reyclebin began calling out names and explaining the color choices as Clombic handed out the suits.

"Punt... blue and white, which depict your focused attention and the ability to communicate." The suit was predominately royal blue with wide, white stripes from the shoulder to the cuffs, a white collar, and white piping along the seams. It felt like a synthetic, stretchy fabric and he imagined it would be like a second skin.

"Veda... soft green, purple, and blue for global healing." She instantly loved it with the solid purple background and varying sizes of green and blue polka dots.

"Frink... blue and coral for your friendliness."

"We wear these under our normal clothing, right?" Frinkle asked as he took his out of wrapping and looked it over. It would definitely be a tight fit if it wasn't stretchable.

"Yes, Frink. You may wear them alone or with other clothing over them. It is your choice," Reyclebin replied before handing out the next suit.

"Portamer... red, brown, green, and yellow for your grounded and clear thinking – giving us reality boosts." The yellow and red ran like rivers between random patches of green and brown – giving it the feel of a patchwork quilt.

"Wow! You will blend in anywhere with those colors, Port!" Frinkle had no problems saying what he was thinking. His main problem was speaking *before* he stopped to think. Portamer grunted a reply that Frinkle couldn't understand and Reyclebin continued as if nothing had been said.

"Limmy... orange, green, and blue to represent your creativity. Oh, there's a little bit of pink thrown in per your request," Reyclebin winked as he handed her suit to her and saw the smile of thanks. Whoever said "orange is the new pink" didn't like pink as much as Limdon. The main cloth was pink. Scattered randomly were different geometric shapes that reminded her of crystals in various stages of growth. The pink matched the color of her fur so closely that it would almost look like she was wearing only the colorful designs. Pumbint raised an eyebrow when he realized this as well.

"Mark... red and yellow for the courage to stand up for what you believe." Red and yellow diagonal stripes in varying widths made his suit unique.

"Beeb... blue and yellow for your written communication and chance for adventure." He was excited that his was yellow with blue stars all over it. The sparkle in his eyes was all Reyclebin needed to know how Beeb felt.

"Cloe... brown and green with a touch of yellow representing your physical strength." While her colors were similar to Portamer's, her pattern was slightly different. Instead of random patchwork shapes, hers were all tri-angles. The yellow on Portamer's was bright-er than the pale yellow used on Clombic's suit. He needed the extra brightness... maybe it would help his demeanor.

"Pader, we have one for you as well... indigo and lavender for your clarity and intuition to guide us on this mission." While indigo and lavender are close in the color spectrum, the indigo holds more blue.

"And lastly, mine is royal purple and fuchsia for wisdom as leader of this mission." His purple suit sported a wide diagonal stripe from the right shoulder to the left hip making it look like a sash. Observing everyone's expressions, he felt good. The suits were expertly designed to encompass each color.

"The significance of these suits is not just the color," Reyclebin continued. "They are specially designed with climate control features to maintain your body temperature at your normal levels - regardless of the Earth's temperature. They also contain gravitational aspects that adjust to the Earth's gravitational pull - which will allow you to walk amongst the humans without feeling weighted down. These are prototypes and you are the first to test them. Let me know immediately if you have any problems."

\* \* \* \* \*

Limdon had worked with Pumbint to integrate the illusion crystal with the coms unit so there would be only one item for each member to wear. The illusion crystal was actually a group of stones and crystals (chosen for their protection and energy properties) fashioned into a circle and placed in the center of the coms unit. Limdon was quite pleased with herself for the design and choices she had made.

"At the center of the circle is malachite in the shape of a star..."

"Sorry I'm late," Frinkle said as he rushed in and took a seat. Limdon had already started the demonstration, but he didn't miss much. He took the sample coms unit as it was passed to him and Limdon continued.

"Malachite is the stone that will allow you to be seen as human because of its visionary power. The stone occupying the top right corner between the first and second points of the star is clear quartz. Clear quartz is a self-energy generator so it will hold the energy to operate the coms unit and the locator. Red jasper fills the lower right corner between the second and third points of the star. It is a stabilizer that helps to balance out the energies and emotional stress.

"The bottom triangle is blue opal. It has a reputation of giving a feeling of invisibility – thus lending strength to the malachite and allowing you to blend in with other beings.    Carnelian fills the lower left area. With its general purpose and feel-better properties, it promotes energy and focus.    It also acts as a backup energy reserve for the clear quartz.

"Turquoise finishes out the circle for three reasons:  First, it is a direct link to the command center on the ship, so it provides a two-way radio function.  Just touch the turquoise to activate telepathic communication; second, it acts as a homing device – in case there are any problems – so the command center can find and rescue if necessary; and third, it is a protection stone that will help keep you safe from accidents while traveling.  Connecting everything together is silver, which is also an energy conductor. It will keep the crystals and stones charged while also providing a power link to the coms unit."

"Do you have any questions?" Pumbint asked.

"Ummm. Yeah.  How am I supposed to wear it?"  Beeb asked.  The piece Limdon demonstrated was designed to be worn like a collar, but Beeb did not have a typical neck. He looked like a big star-shaped sponge with hands and feet.  The center part of the star (which is his head) was an independent circle that rotated on a vertical axis. He could reverse directions without turning his whole body – just his head.

"Actually, Beeb, we thought of the challenges some of the members may have due to their various body shapes. That's why we have two styles. You will be able to wear yours like a wrist watch." Pumbint explained as Limdon fastened one to his wrist.

Beeb smiled his thanks to Pumbint. He turned his chair back toward the front of the cabin and saw Morach sulking in the corner. He wondered what could have him down before they even landed. *Is something wrong? Are we walking (or flying) into a trap?* Now Beeb was concerned as well.

"Our destination is coming into view, Sir... I mean, Rey" Pader informed Reyclebin. "Everyone should buckle down and return their chairs to their locked positions as we prepare for landing." As they were already seated, fastening the safety harnesses was a quick task.

After applying his own harness, Reyclebin got their attention once more. "When we land, you will need to take a few minutes to adjust to the gravity and put on your suits. The entryway that you came through upon boarding is a decompression (or compression) and disinfecting chamber if necessary. It can hold all of us at one time if needed, but smaller groups are best. It takes only a minute to decompress, even though you may think it would take longer. Your suits will aid in the decompression process. And don't forget to wear your coms unit at all times, which Limmy and Punt have demonstrated."

Their faces held looks of concern behind masks of bravery. Nobody wanted to admit they were a little afraid. Now that they were actually in Earth's atmosphere, the reality of the mission finally took hold. *Would they find happiness on Earth?*

## Beeb's First Report

Galactic Day 1 –

*I'm not exactly sure what I am doing here. I have been given the job of record keeper and am supposed to write a report of our progress in finding happiness after each Earth week. However, we have just entered Earth's atmosphere safely and will dock soon – but I don't really have anything to report at this time. So, I will write about what happened during our flight.*

*We introduced ourselves and found we have several experts on our team. Vedagy may be only three and one-half feet tall, but she can cook! Some members have special dietary needs and she meets them all… from vegetarian for her, to total carnivorous for Clombic, to all things sugar for Portamer, and strictly liquids for Mr. President. It's a good thing most of us can have a combination of the special dishes so she doesn't have to cook a whole menu for every meal.*

It is hard to believe sweet, gentle Clombic is a lethal weapon. She is at least six – if not seven – feet tall, has three legs that take over half her height (her legs are taller than Vedagy!), three arms, and her head is slender and cylindrical with a flat nose and ears. Her one eye rotates all the way around so she can see in any direction. I suppose that would be an advantage when you can see your opponents coming from anywhere. I hope we don't need to find out how good she is.

Morach seems melancholy although it is difficult to tell because his one large eyelid has been half closed most of the time I've known him. He is big and bulky and could probably squeeze the wind out of someone with his muscular arms. He kept to himself during most of the trip. I think he is blaming himself for the possible takeover of Earth. I hope he finds the answers he needs and we find enough happiness to save this planet.

There is something about Limdon and Pumbint. They seem to be really good friends and work well together. When they were showing us how to use the coms units, they finished each other's sentences. They are smart, though, and I'm sure they can fix anything if something goes wrong with the ship. Let's hope it doesn't.

Portamer is very formal. He refuses to use anyone's nicknames. I wonder if he even knows what *happiness looks like. It is fitting that, as a professor, he has three eyes and wears glasses...it gives him a very studious look.*

*Frinkle is funny. I think he and I will be great friends. He doesn't even have to use the transformation part of the coms unit because he can pass as human. He doesn't have fur like Pumbint and Limdon, just a light dusting of hair on his arms and legs and a healthy crop of red hair on his head. He has spots all over his body. I think someone called them freckles. His ears have a little bit of a point to them, but if he keeps them covered, he will blend in just fine... or so I'm told.*

*Reyclebin is our esteemed leader. The reason he has to have a diet of liquids is that he is made up mostly of water. On his planet, most Bolcusans are tall and slender while some are short and wide. We have people on our planet that make animals out of long, skinny balloons for the ailing. Reyclebin reminds me of one of those balloons filled with water with the tied end as a sort of tail and, if the balloon wasn't blown up all the way to the end, the tip of the balloon is his nose and his two eyes are on separate tentacles like antennae. But, of course, if you are from Bolcus, you already know this. I think it's cool that he can walk on his hands and feet (I think they are called mitts) or just his back feet.*

Oh, we also got special jumpsuits that are supposed to help regulate our body heat – regardless of how hot or cold it is. Vedagy explained to me that our moods are influenced by the colors we wear, which is why our suits are made of special colors – to help us do our specialized jobs. Mine will help me write and add to my new adventure, giving me the boost I need to get over my shyness… I hope.

Well, I think that takes care of our trip. We are getting ready to land, so I will write again tomorrow.

This concludes my report for galactic day one of the mission to Search for Happiness and Assess the Destiny of Earth.

## two

## *Arriving on Earth*

"Frinkle!"

"Frankle!" The boys embraced in a brotherly hug to show their excitement in being reunited. "It's so good to see you again!" Frankle moved from Pluto to Earth several years ago when Pluto started dissolving – it is no longer the planet it once was. He has been working for Mr. Hardgold as his travel secretary since his arrival. Frinkle, his cousin, contacted him a couple of days ago and asked if he knew where they could stay during their five-week visit. Frankle immediately told him about Mr. Hardgold's hotels around the world and offered to let the visitors stay in them. They agreed to discuss the itinerary during the first half of their Earth week. The first stop in their quest to find happiness on Earth brought them to New York, New York, in the United States of America.

"Let me introduce my friends. This is Reyclebin...or Rey. He is our fearless leader," Frinkle said with a smile that said he was trying to earn points with the boss. "This little one here is Veda. She has a lot of energy, so we try to keep a leash on her. Oops! Sorry, Veda. Here we have Pumbint, or Punt, who is our electronics expert, and Limmy is our crystal energy expert. This is Mark our conflict analyst. Beeb is our record keeper. And this tall, lanky dame is our weapons expert, Cloe. Never would have guessed it, eh?" Frinkle knew the look he received from her meant he better keep himself in line, but the sparkle in her eye reminded him she was a sweetheart and wouldn't actually hurt him. "And, finally, we have Portamer. What can I say about Portamer? He is basically our skeptic and the resident downer. Just kidding, Port, old man." Portamer growled at Frinkle – emphasizing the correctness of his introduction.

"So, there you have it. Nice group, eh? Everyone, this is my cousin, Frankle."

When Frankle finished shaking hands with everyone, he noticed the first balloon

floating by. "Oh! You are just in time for the parade! Every year, Macy's department store hosts a parade on Thanksgiving Day with floats, balloons, bands, and lots of food and fun. Come on over to the edge to take a closer look!"

There was a three-foot retaining wall around the roof to protect anyone from falling over the edge and down twenty-six stories to the street. They could just see the balloons beginning to float past. Vedagy was having a little difficulty seeing because of her height, so Frankle lifted her onto a chair that had been left on the rooftop. She leaned against the ledge to see the sights.

"It's so noisy."

"Are those humans down there?"

"You called these balloons. They are quite large. How do they stay afloat with the gravity factor?"

The chatter continued with everyone talking at once. Frankle attempted to answer some of the questions starting with Portamer's gravity question. "The balloons are filled with a helium gas which allows them to defy gravity. They are attached to cables to control how high they can climb, so they don't float away and can be pulled down at the end of the parade. They have a valve to release the gas so the balloons can be packed and used again the following year." Turning to Portamer, he asked, "Does that answer your question?"

Portamer nodded, "Thank you. That was a sufficient explanation. I believe I understand how they operate now."

"Can we go see the humans?" Beeb asked. He asked it so quietly he had to repeat it twice for anyone to hear him. It's sometimes a nuisance being so shy. Writing is so much easier for Beeb because he can let himself go without feeling judged.

"If you like, we can go to your rooms which are on the third floor. Normally, the penthouse suite would be used, but it is undergoing renovations at the moment and I thought the third floor may be a good viewing point. Of course, once you are settled, we can go down to the street if you want. Since this is your first day, you might want to meet the people slowly."

"We are on a limited time table, Frankle, but I do agree that we should ease into this just a little. This gravity is pulling my body into strange shapes, though I would like to get a closer look at the humans to gauge their happiness levels. Please lead the way."

"Of course, Rey, follow me. Just a word, though? The humans are referred to as people here on Earth. You will want to blend in as much as possible, so calling them humans in their presence would sound odd to them. Also, I go by Frank here. It is more of a human name. Please enter the elevator and we will go to your rooms."

Upon reaching the third floor, Frankle led the group to a four-bedroom suite that was often used for business conferences. It had a living room area with large windows, two sofas that housed fold-out beds, two arm chairs, a coffee table laden with flowers and magazines, end tables with candy dishes filled with mints, artificial fichus trees in the corners, and a decorative chandelier hanging from the center of the ceiling.

To the left of the living room stood a full kitchen on two walls with a breakfast bar to form a perfect triangle. Four leather-covered bar stools were pushed up against the oak siding. A well-stocked beverage cooler sat beneath the counter on the kitchen side of the bar. Serving dishes, utensils, cookware, glasses, and storage containers filled the cupboards. Limited spices and seasonings were also provided. Under normal circumstances, the suite was not stocked with food; but Frankle took the liberty of doing some grocery shopping, so there was enough food for a week. He just hoped they liked his selections.

Across from the kitchen sat a large dining table with a picture-perfect fruit bowl centerpiece and eight high-backed chairs neatly standing around it. A potted plant sat in the corner. Beautiful, oak-framed, French-style doors led onto a balcony that ran the length of the dining room. Sliding-glass doors in the living room also accessed the balcony.

Beeb, Frinkle, and Vedagy saw the balcony at the same time and headed straight outside. The rail around the balcony allowed Vedagy to view the festivities between the bars. From this height, they could see the floats and the cables attached to the balloons flying above their heads. They could see the smiles on the spectators bordering the parade. There were people crowding the sidewalks on either side of the street as far as the eye could see – and they were all smiling and laughing.

"Rey, Portamer, Mark, over here! You've all got to see this! I think we've found happiness!"

"I highly doubt that, Veda, but let us take a look," Portamer replied. Skeptic that he was, he was unaffected by their excitement. "What makes you believe they are happy?"

"It's so obvious, Portamer," Beeb, forgetting his shyness, chimed in. "They are all smiling and laughing and waving at each other. How can you think they aren't happy?"

"Happiness is more than superficial actions, Beeb. It comes from within one's soul and is found in acts of kindness. Merely laughing and carrying on is not indicative of true happiness."

"Very well put, Portamer. It is our position to obtain proof of happiness and an elaborate festival does not provide proof. We can enjoy the festivities, go down to the street to meet some of the people and look for acts of kindness that spread actual happiness."

"Thank you, Sir."

"Wow, what a downer," Frinkle said. "Did I not tell you, Frank, that he could be a downer?"

"Frinkle, you know he is correct,"

Reyclebin chastised.

"Yeah, I know, Sir. But can't we have a little fun while we're here?" Frinkle hung his head. "How long does the parade last, Frank?"

"It usually runs about three hours. It started about an hour ago, so a couple more hours, I'd say."

"Very well, you may enjoy the remainder of the parade on one condition. If you leave this room, you must stay together and Cloe must accompany you. Cloe, you are the one trained in defensive arts in case anything should arise. Remember, though, you are NOT to instigate anything in any way. Violence is not something we want to find in our pursuit of happiness," Reyclebin stated the rules. While allowing for fun and frolicking, he charged them with a sense of responsibility and named Clombic their guardian and protector. "I would like to see the bed chambers now, Frank. I fear this gravity is bringing my age to bear."

On Bolcus, the gravitational pull is half the strength of Earth's, so Reyclebin was beginning to droop and change his shape from long and cylindrical to short and stubby,

resembling a drop of water. This made walking on all four limbs difficult; and his balance on two limbs, with the shifted weight, would take getting used to before he could walk normally.

"Right this way, Sir."

They re-entered the suite through the living room and turned to the left. Two bedrooms were on one side of the suite and shared a large bathroom, while the other two bedrooms were on the other side of the suite and shared the other bath. A master bedroom was not designed into this suite due to the nature of the regular clientele: business executives.

"In here, Sir." Frankle led Reyclebin into the bedroom facing the street.

"I think I'd prefer the room away from the street if you don't mind, Frank. The noise from the celebration may be a bit of a distraction from rest."

"Of course. What was I thinking? We can go through the bathroom. You see we have a whirlpool tub in each bathroom as well as a shower stall and the usual facilities separated by a shorter wall. Here we are." A queen-sized bed, two nightstands with side lamps, dresser, desk with small lamp, and a desk chair filled the room. A large closet was on the same wall as the door leading to the living room, providing an extra buffer from noise.

"Thank you, Frank. You are a gracious and generous host. I will see you again this afternoon."

"You are very welcome, Sir. Have a restful sleep." Frankle closed the bathroom door and the door to the living area on his way out.

"Pimbint is it?"

"Pumbint, but please call me Punt."

"Right. Sorry. He didn't look too good. Is he going to be okay?"

"I'm sure he'll be fine; but I'll stay here and stand watch while he rests. Thank you for your concern." He patted Frankle on the shoulder and turned to the others.

"If you are going to enjoy the rest of the parade, you should get going. I'll stay here in case Rey needs anything. Keep it down, now; we don't want to wake him." Pumbint shooed them out the door then went to find a snack.

When Reyclebin emerged from the bedroom an hour later, he found Pumbint lying on the couch on his back, snoring, with one foot on the floor and an apple core dangling from between the fingers of the arm sticking out over the edge. Reyclebin smiled and headed to the kitchen for a glass of water. Hearing the ice machine in the door of the refrigerator, Pumbint roused from his noisy slumber.

"Oh. Hello, Sir," he mumbled through his yawn and stretch.

"Hello, yourself. I see you were elected to stay behind... or did you volunteer so you could recoup as well?"

Blushing, Pumbint replied, "Uh, I just wanted to be here in case you needed something, Sir. I guess I fell asleep after my snack. How are you feeling?"

"I'm feeling much better, thank you. Is the parade still going by? It sounds a bit quieter." He and Pumbint ambled toward the balcony. The parade was still in progress but the crowds had thinned a little. "Do you want to go down to the street? We can stay close to the hotel until the others return."

"I'd like that. Are you feeling up to it?"

"I'm fine, Punt. Stop fussing."

"Look. I think I see Cloe. She has Veda on her shoulders," he laughed at the sight. "You can't miss them."

"They do present a delightful picture, don't they? Come, let's join them."

"I saw them this direction. There they are!" Pumbint and Reyclebin moved through the crowd toward the rest of the committee members.

"Hi! Did you have a good rest, Sir?" Vedagy greeted them as they drew near.

"Yes, I did, Veda, thank you for asking. I see you have found a better vantage point. Are you enjoying yourself?" he said with a wink and a smile.

"Yes, Sir. We saw lots of balloons and cars with flowers on them – they call them floats because they look like they're floating even though they are really just cars. At least, that's what Frank told us. We even had some sweet, hot liquid they call cocoa. It warmed us right up!"

"Excuse me, Sir," a woman held a warm blanket out towards Reyclebin. "I couldn't help noticing you are turning a little blue from the cold. I'd like to offer you this blanket to help warm you up… No, no, I don't need it," she said when Reyclebin tried to refuse it. "My son and I are on our way home and you need it worse than we do."

"Very well. I thank you kind lady." Reyclebin took the blanket and Clombic helped wrap it around him.

"It is my pleasure. I am happy to see you will be warm." The lady and her son moved on through the crowds.

"That was very kind of that lady to give ya the blanket, Sir. She seemed truly happy to give it to ya." Clombic's southern drawl was ever present.

"Yes. Yes she did, didn't she? You know, Cloe, I think we may have just witnessed a bit of happiness on Earth. It doesn't mean we should stop our mission, but I have seen a spark." He smiled as they continued watching the parade.

Vedagy realized Reyclebin had been very quiet for the past half hour. He wasn't commenting on the floats or balloons with the rest of them. She looked at him and the blanket had slipped from his shoulders. He was very blue and not moving.

"Sir?" Alarmed, she nudged Clombic. "What's wrong with Rey?"

"What, Veda? I couldn't hear ya." The parade was over but everyone was chattering, which made it difficult to hear. Vedagy pointed behind them. She turned and saw Reyclebin. "Oh no! Punt, Frinkle, hey, we need some help over here!" She shouted above the din at the males to help her. "We need to carry him to our suite as quickly as possible. He's frozen solid!"

They wrapped him in the blanket and carried him back to the hotel suite. When they got there, Frankle started a lukewarm bath to help thaw Reyclebin. Little by little, he began to look like himself again. They removed the crystal so they could see how he was really doing. He would have melted into a puddle if it weren't for his skin holding him together.

"Oh my! What happened?" Reyclebin asked as he thawed and was able to talk again.

After Reyclebin was fully recovered, the team held a brief conference. They decided he would spend the remaining weeks in the motel rooms or aboard the ship, where the captain could control the environment, or he would not survive. Something must have malfunctioned in his suit because it wasn't doing its job. Five weeks exposed to Earth's atmosphere would be too long for Reyclebin. He was 65 galactic years of age, which made him 480 Earth years. The fact that Reyclebin was 90% water put him at higher risk because of the pull of the moon and the cold weather. He had already frozen into an ice cube and melted into a puddle in the first day.

Fortunately, he had seen the Macy's Thanksgiving Day parade and witnessed the joy the humans shared while they gathered in the streets. He was already convinced there was happiness on Earth and was content to spend the remainder of their mission aboard the ship. He would be the home-base commander and manage the communications center.

The ship was still on the rooftop where it would remain until they departed for their next point of interest. After escorting Reyclebin to the ship and speaking with the captain, the team was assured that Reyclebin would be fine. Everyone agreed to meet at the ship in a few days to see how he was feeling.

"Very well, I will take this time to catch up on some much needed rest. Don't worry about me. I will contact you if anything arises. Go find your version of happiness on Earth."

# Communication (Coms) Unit

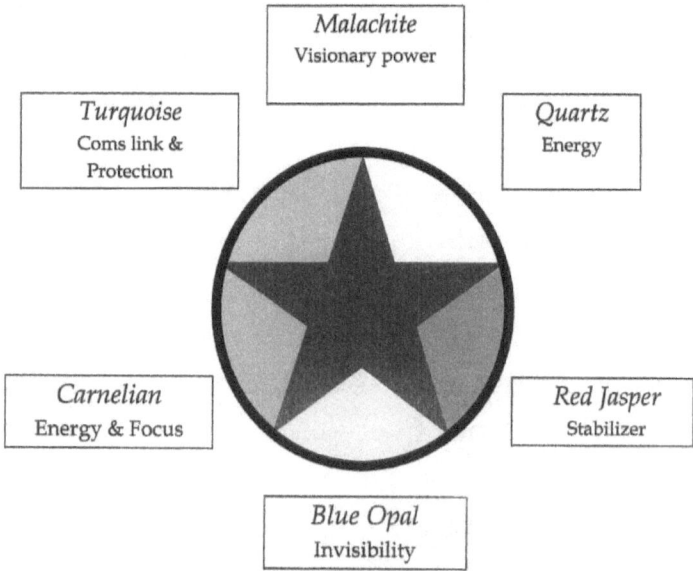

**Malachite**
Visionary power

**Turquoise**
Coms link &
Protection

**Quartz**
Energy

**Carnelian**
Energy & Focus

**Red Jasper**
Stabilizer

**Blue Opal**
Invisibility

## three

## *Tony*

"I know you want to be here in case Rey needs us, Portamer, and I'm concerned about him, too. But you know I don't eat meat like the rest of you so I need to get some vegetables," Vedagy stated. "Everyone else will be here if Rey needs anything and, quite honestly, there isn't anything we can do that they can't."

"Are you forgetting that Frank purchased a wide variety of food in anticipation of our tastes? Did you not find anything to satisfy your vegetarian palate?" Portamer asked.

"No, I didn't. It's not that I am ungrateful, but I need stuff to make a nice salad and we just don't have it. Could you go with me? It will take only a few minutes," Vedagy pleaded.

"We do not have any currency. How do you propose we pay for this additional food?"

"Frank said we could put it on his account. We just tell the man at the counter it is for Mr. Hardgold and Frank sent us to pick it up. I even have directions. It's just a few blocks down and one block over. It's called Garden Eats," she informed him with a smile. "If we hurry, we can be back before the lasagna is done."

"All right. I will inform Cloe we are taking our leave."

While he was talking to Clombic and assuring her they didn't need her protection, Morach was asking if he could go along for some fresh air. Vedagy asked Beeb to take the lasagna out of the oven in 30 minutes, if they weren't back by then, so it could rest before dinner.

Morach, Portamer and Vedagy took a left when they exited the hotel. Vedagy ooohed and ahhhed as she saw the various fashions and furniture staged in the big, store-front windows. She liked the pretty humanoid clothing. She wondered how they would look on her human figure. The jumpsuits issued to the committee members were protective and comfortable enough, but they didn't have any style to show individuality – only color. She chose a majestic purple because it was her favorite color and looked good against her silvery skin. Of course, nobody could see her silver skin-tone and gourd-shaped body because the crystal Limdon had given each member gave the illusion of a human form. Still, she could dream about how some of the dresses would look on her.

Portamer was his usual self – intent on getting to their destination and not wanting to interact with the humans. He was here to observe, not to enjoy himself. He was chosen to come on this mission because he is a professor of anthropology and a skeptic. He didn't believe they would find true happiness on Earth. *Why engage with these humans when they will be destroyed anyway*, he thought.

Morach, however, was focused on the humans. He felt responsible for Earth almost getting destroyed without this close-up study. He was the lead on the scouting team; and the data they collected from the Earth's satellites was filled with anger, meanness, and general negativity. Just from what he had seen thus far, he knew they didn't have complete information with the satellite data. The guilt was eating at him, which was why he had been so quiet since they left the docking station. He had to find out where all that negativity came from.

"It's just ahead," Vedagy said, breaking into their thoughts. The boys didn't even register that they had made the two turns already. They were on auto pilot and Vedagy was in control. "Wow! This is a great store. Look at the variety!" She started filling a basket with different vegetables: butter lettuce, leaf lettuce, Indian lettuce, kale, radishes, green onions, peppers, and spinach. She noticed rice vinegar, olive oil, and spices at the hotel, so she didn't need to get anything for a dressing. She had enough to make two large salads that would serve everyone. As she headed toward the counter, the shopkeeper started yelling at a young boy trying to steal an apple.

Morach was closest and caught the boy before he could leave. The shopkeeper retrieved the apple with a chastisement to the boy then turned to help Vedagy (who had added an apple to her bounty). While she was talking to the shopkeeper, Morach questioned the still struggling boy. "Where are your parents?"

"I don't have any. Let me go!"

"What's your name?"

"What's it to you? Let me go!"

"Tell me your name and I'll give you this apple," Vedagy said as she walked over and held up the apple she had just purchased.

"Tony. Now give me the apple," he said as he reached for it.

"How would you like to have some lasagna?" Vedagy asked. "You could come with us, have dinner and get warm. You look hungry." Portamer gave her a look that said he didn't approve, but he didn't voice his concern.

"Okay, I guess. I do like lasagna."

"Good! I am Veda, this is Mark, and this is Portamer. We're staying at the Surtic Hotel just a few blocks away. Come, take my hand." They walked hand-in-hand back to the hotel in silence.

"Hi, everyone," Vedagy said as they entered the suite. "I brought a guest to dinner."

"Ahhh, I see you've met Tony," Frankle, said. "I often buy him an apple when I go to market. How are you today, Tony? Keeping warm?"

"Hi, Frank. I'm fine, thank you. Sure am glad to see a face I know. Not that these guys weren't nice and all. Where's dinner?"

Snickers were heard throughout the group. "I took the lasagna out of the oven a few minutes ago, Veda."

"Thanks, Beeb. I'll put this salad together quickly, and then we can eat. Can someone set the table? Oh! We have ten people and eight places."

"Punt and I will sit on the balcony to eat, if it's okay. That will even out the seating," Limdon said. "And I've already set the tables. I'll just add a place for Tony."

"Won't it be too cold out?" Frinkle asked.

"No, we'll be fine. We run to the warm side and our suits are working fine." Pumbint answered.

"Here we are. Lasagna, salad, and bread sticks. Beverages are in the cooler under the counter. Help yourselves. Cloe, I made a steak just for you."

"This is good, Veda," Tony complimented. "It's a little different, but I like it."

"I used spinach lasagna noodles. I usually make it without the meat, but these guys get a little cranky without it."

"So, Tony, where do you live?" asked Clombic.

"Here and there. I don't really have a home right now."

"Where are your parents?"

"They died in a car crash a few months ago," he said as tears pooled in his eyes.

"Do you attend school?" Portamer asked.

"No, I've been hiding out. Nobody even noticed I'm not there. I think they figured I died in the accident, too. I don't really have any friends and I don't have any relatives. Basically, I'm on my own."

"If you could have anything you wanted, what would fill you with happiness?" Morach asked.

"That's easy, Mark. I want to be an elf for Santa," Tony promptly replied with a big smile, quickly recovering from his sadness.

"Who is this Santa and what is an elf?" Portamer asked.

"What?! You don't know who Santa is? What planet are you from?" Tony exclaimed. Blank looks appeared on everyone's faces as they put their hands on their crystals – activating the telepathic coms unit.

*Does he know? How could he? Did somebody's crystal stop working? How are we supposed to answer this? This is a question for Rey. Why did Veda bring this Earthling to our inner sanctum?* The thoughts were flying.

Tony looked right back at their blank faces with surprise on his. "Oh, you have to be kidding! Okay. Let me tell you about Santa. He is mostly called Santa Claus or St. Nicholas and is called other names in other countries. He wears a red and white suit, has a white beard, knows when you've been good or bad, sees you when you're sleeping, and spreads happiness to everyone on Christmas Day."

"He sounds kind of scary – knowing everything about everyone," whispered Beeb with a frown on his face.

"Oh, no. He's a jolly old fellow. I remember asking Santa for a red wagon when I was little and on Christmas morning I found it under the Christmas tree with a big red ribbon." Tony's eyes lit up with the memory.

"So what is this elf you aspire to be?" Portamer asked.

"Santa has a workshop where the elves build the toys for him to deliver on Christmas Eve. The elves are short like me and Veda, have pointed ears (almost like Frinkle and Frank), wear green elf suits, and some take care of Santa's reindeer, too. They are happy

 44

all the time and I want to be happy, too."

"Where can we find this Santa?" Frinkle asked.

"Well, the real Santa is at his workshop at the north pole. At least, that's how the stories go. I haven't met the real Santa... yet... that I know of, anyway. But he has lots of helpers. The malls have Santa helpers dressed up just like Santa and all the kids take turns sitting on his lap and telling him what they want for Christmas. The real Santa sometimes sits in, so you never know if it's the real Santa or one of his helpers that you are visiting. It's really cool and everyone is always so happy."

"Frank, can you take us to see Santa?" Vedagy asked.

"I will find out when he will be in town and get back to you on that," Frank replied.

"Tony, do you have a warm place to stay?" Limdon asked, entering the suite with the dishes from the balcony.

"I usually grab a bunk at the mission, but it's too late to find one for tonight."

"You can stay here tonight, then. Beeb, can he bunk with you?" Limdon suggested.

"Sure, not a problem. I think I'll head to bed now. Which room is ours?" Beeb asked.

That just brought up another series of problems, though. Where was everyone to sleep? They were now back to nine bodies and six beds. Beeb and Tony took the front bedroom off the kitchen. Frankle brought in a roll-a-way bed for Vedagy, which they put in the room next to Tony and Beeb. Limdon would take the bed and Clombic would take the closet because it had a bar she could sleep on. That left Pumbint in the room Reyclebin had used, Portamer in the front room, and Frinkle and Morach on the sofa beds.

After they cleaned up the kitchen, they went to their respective rooms for the night and dreamt about finding happiness. Would it be this Santa person? Or was he just another superficial happiness? This was just the beginning. There was so much more to learn.

## four

## *Seeking Santa*

"We have been to seven malls over the past five days and have not located the genuine Santa. I am not impressed by the imposters we have seen. Yes, people seem to be in good spirits, but it is not overwhelming evidence in my opinion. Our time in this city ends tomorrow and we have made little progress. I suggest we meet with Reyclebin to debrief and plan our next phase of this mission," Portamer announced.

"I agree, but I need to make one short excursion before we leave. Punt, would you escort me?" Limdon asked.

"My pleasure," he replied. "When do you want to leave?"

"I need to see Rey alone for a minute then we can go."

"Okay. I'll be right here when you are ready."

"Thanks. I'll be back in fifteen minutes,"

she told him.  Limdon went to the elevator and pressed the up button.  She knew they were going to other parts of the world and Frankle wouldn't be there to help them with finances.  She had asked around and located a jeweler that would pay top dollar for a flawless sapphire – especially the size she had in mind.  Her meeting with Reyclebin was just a ruse to retrieve the stone.  She would, of course, let Reyclebin know what she was doing but knew he would not object.  Clombic, on the other hand, would object when she found out how much money she would be carrying without asking for her protective escort.

Nobody was on the elevator.  If anyone boarded, she would act like she was going to the top floor.  They didn't need anyone finding the ship on the roof.  Pumbint was a great engineer.  She smiled at how well they work together.  He made modifications to the ship that would let people think it was a helicopter (for landing on rooftops), a motor home or bus for travel on land, or an airplane to cross the ocean.  It could even transform into a houseboat if necessary.  Her crystals powered it, though, so they never had to purchase fuel.

Safely on the rooftop, Limdon approached the ship. The captain lowered the hatch as she reached it.

"Hello, Captain. How have you been?" she asked politely.

"I'm good, thank you, Limmy. Rey is expecting you."

Entering the decontamination chamber, Limdon held out her arms for the antibacterial spray. This is just a precaution so they don't take any germs back to their galaxies. "Hello, Rey. How have you been faring up here with the captain? I apologize we haven't been here more often."

"I'm doing well, Limmy. I couldn't handle the Earth's climate. I didn't anticipate that minor issue."

"We all understand, Sir. It actually works out that you can be kept safe while having the opportunity to have the ship moved if it becomes compromised; and you can communicate with everyone via the coms center."

"True. Thanks for cheering me up. So where is everyone else?"

"Oh, they'll be up soon for a debriefing. I'm here because I need to speak with you alone for a moment." As she explained her idea, she located the sapphire and continued. "I anticipated the need for currency during our stay, so I brought along a flawless gemstone I thought the humans would purchase. I did some research and found a local jeweler of high reputation who is willing to pay a great sum for this gem. Punt will accompany me – although, he is unaware of my plan at the moment. The others don't know, either."

"It seems you have thought this out. I am pleased that you are prepared, yet I wonder why you did not discuss this with me before we left home base," he commented with concern in his voice.

"I apologize, Sir, but I didn't want to get our hopes up if I was unsuccessful in finding a buyer. I didn't want to fail you."

"You did not fail me and I would not have blamed you if a buyer was not found. However, it is a brave thing you do. I sense that stone has some meaning for you?"

"Yes, Sir. My mother gave it to me when I started my crystals and gemstones training. But, it is for a good cause. Frank won't be with us and should not fulfill our monetary needs. This is what I wish to do."

"Very well. Be careful. You should take

Cloe with you, but I know you won't."

"No, Sir. I would prefer not to take her. This is personal for me."

"Okay. Go. Report back here when you complete your task."

"Yes, Sir. I will send the others for debriefing. Thank you, Sir."

With the exception of Limdon and Pumbint, the committee members assembled at the ship. After each member went through the decontamination chamber, they greeted Reyclebin and took their seats. Because they were safely concealed in the ship, they turned off their crystals for a chance to be in their natural shapes and sizes. It was nice to finally relax even if it was for only a few minutes. Everyone was wondering where Limdon and Pumbint went in such secrecy. Reyclebin wasn't telling them anything except that the two would return soon.

"Is everyone comfortable?" Reyclebin asked.

"Yes, Sir," they replied.

"Very well. Where do we stand on the search for happiness? Cloe, you may begin,"

"We have met a young Earth boy who aspires to be Santa's elf. Apparently this Santa person spreads happiness around the world. We visited several shopping malls where Santa was reportedly visiting and, while they were only his helpers, everyone seemed full of joy to speak with him. People were buying gifts to give others in the spirit of spreading the happiness," she supplied.

"So would you say you have found that there is happiness here?" Reyclebin asked.

"Sir, if I may," inserted Portamer. "While we've seen some people being happy, I am not yet convinced of this selfless giving of sincere happiness. I think we need to look further. We are told this Santa resides at the north pole and suggest we go there next."

"Very well, Portamer. Do you all feel the same way?"

"I think he's right that we should go to the north pole," Frinkle chimed in, "but there's something I'd like to propose. Tony is an orphan, the one who told us about Santa, and is all alone living on the streets. I was wondering if he could come with us. Before you say no – I see the look in your eyes, Portamer – I think it would be a chance for us to help spread a little of this happiness we are pursuing."

"There are so many things wrong with that idea, Frinkle..."

"I think it's a great idea!" Vedagy interrupted Morach. "He has a lot of spirit and I think he can help us on our mission."

"But, Veda... Frinkle... what about him seeing us in our natural state – or seeing our ship? We aren't from this planet. How can we bring in a human and maintain our secret identities?" Reyclebin responded with concern in his voice.

"Sir, if I may?" Beeb asked. "I shared a room with Tony this week. He went everywhere with us and helped us understand some of Earth's ways. He may be only fourteen Earth years, but he is full of wisdom and can be a helpful guide. I truly think we can trust him without him freaking out." This was the longest speech Beeb had given on the whole trip.

"Beeb, I don't think I've heard you say so much at one time. I'd like to meet this Tony before I make the final decision," Reyclebin responded. "I will come down to the suite." He held up his hands at their concerned objections. "I won't stay long. If you recall, I was fine for the first few hours. I promise I will meet Tony then return to the ship. Is he in the suite now?"

"Yes, Sir, he is," answered Portamer. "I would like to go on record as protesting this proposed endeavor."

"So noted, Portamer. Now, let us go meet Tony."

Tony had no idea of the possibility he could be joining the group on the rest of their mission. He was waiting in the suite while the committee was having a meeting. He didn't know why they couldn't just meet at the dining room table unless the meeting was about him. They were supposed to leave tomorrow, so he was feeling a little sad. It was really nice spending the week with them – eating good meals, looking for Santa, having a warm place to sleep. He really liked these people. They were different, but different was good. *Oh, it sounds like they're back.*

The group was chattering as they entered the suite, then stopped when they saw Tony. Most of them wore smiles as they gathered in the living area and took their places on the sofas.

"Tony, please join us. This is our committee chairman, Rey. He has come for a short

visit before he prepares our transportation for tomorrow's departure," said Clombic.

"Hello," Tony said shyly as he pulled a chair over from the dining table. "Nice to meet you."

"Hello, Tony. I hear you have been escorting the group around the city this past week."

"Yes, Sir. We've been to all the malls we can find. I'm a little disappointed we couldn't find the real Santa, but I'm sure you will find him on the next part of your journey." Tony said with regret in his voice.

"Tony, do you think there is life on other planets?"

"Oh, yes, Sir! Frank is from another planet isn't he? I knew it! Of course, he never told me, but I just knew it! That is so cool! Which planet is he from...Mars?" Tony replied excitedly.

Chuckling, Reyclebin replied, "No, he is actually from Pluto – as is Frinkle." Some of the committee members gasped that Reyclebin would disclose such a thing. "Of course, you can't tell anyone. We wouldn't want Frank to lose his job, now, would we?"

"Oh, no, Sir! I wouldn't tell anyone – I don't have anyone to tell anyway. Wait.

Didn't I hear that Pluto wasn't a planet?" he asked, puzzled. Before anyone could answer, he continued, "Are you guys from another planet, too? This is awesome!"

"Well, in a literal sense, yes, we are. You are a very intelligent young man, Tony. I am going to share something with you which you must also promise to keep secret, okay?"

"Yes, Sir. No problem," promised Tony.

"Beeb, could you remove your crystal, please?" Reyclebin instructed. Beeb removed his crystal and became visible in his natural form.

"Wow! A star-shaped sponge with a circle in the middle. Can you turn around?" Tony laughed. Beeb rotated his head to the back and took a step, then rotated back to the front and took a step toward Tony. "Cool! You don't even have to turn around to go the other direction." Tony was excited seeing Beeb's natural form. "Does it hurt to have a human body?"

"No, I still feel like I normally do. I think the crystal just makes us look   human," Beeb replied.

"So what do the rest of you look like?" Tony asked.

Seeing Tony's enthusiasm and easy acceptance to their true forms, Reyclebin nodded to everyone to reveal themselves. Tony was awestruck. He had never seen aliens up close before. This was better than having ice cream for dinner every day – which was another dream he had. He would remember this moment forever.

"Tony, you seem a little overwhelmed. Are you okay?" Vedagy asked.

"I'm fine, Veda, I'm just thinking that you will be leaving tomorrow and I just found out you are from other planets. I'm just a little sad, is all," Tony replied with a frown.

"Well, Tony, I have another surprise for you," Reyclebin added. "How would you like to come with us while we travel on Earth? We will be here only four more weeks, but you can join us during that time..."

As soon as Reyclebin said he could go with them, Tony started jumping around yelling, "Yippee!" and hugged each alien. He couldn't have been happier at this moment. He was actually going with them!

"Hey, do you have a space ship, too? Can I see it?" Tony asked excitedly.

"You will see it in due time. Do you have

any belongings you need to pack?" Reyclebin asked.

"No, Sir. I don't have anything. Hey, can I get a cool jumpsuit like you guys have?"

"We'll see what we can find," Morach said. "Welcome to the team."

"Thank you! Thank you! Thank you! I am so excited I won't be able to sleep tonight!" Tony exclaimed. "What time do we leave? Where are we going? Are we going on the ship? What does it look like? Where is it?"

"Tony, chill, dude," Frinkle said laughing. "You'll find out tomorrow. We have to have *some* surprises, ya know."

"Can we go to bed now so it will be tomorrow faster? This is almost like Christmas!" Tony just couldn't settle down. He was about to go on the adventure of his life.

Reyclebin had a smile on his face when he put the crystal back on so he could go back to the ship. He could spend a little time in the Earth's gravity but not long. He promised to see Tony in the morning at the ship. The others would stay in the suite until it was time to go.

* * * * *

"I'll be fine, Falcyn. I'm feeling much better now that I'm onboard. The others are continuing with the mission. You know Portamer, he will be the hardest to convince. I was the first to see this happiness for what it is – true joy that only comes from sharing and giving of oneself without any expectation of return. Of course, Frinkle is excited just to be here and see his cousin again." He had to smile when he thought of how they danced and laughed when they were reunited. They truly were like children.

"I'm sorry, what did you say, dear? Our time is running short. I'm losing the signal. Remember I am fine and will be home in a few galactic days." He didn't have time to say more as the image on the screen faded away.

"Sir, we won't be able to do another communication until next week so the crystals have time to charge again. Earth's sun does not stay lit as long as ours and the power to communicate at that distance is draining."

"I understand, Limdon. You did what you could to let me talk to Falcyn and I don't want to jeopardize the safety of the committee."

"There is ample power to keep you comfortable until next week if we don't communicate with home until then."

\* \* \* \* \*

"Thank you, Frank," Reyclebin began. "We appreciate everything you have done for us. We will keep in touch and let you know when we leave North Pole." The captain had located North Pole on the map. It is located in the state of Alaska – above Canada. The ship would fly them within 40 miles of the town, then change shapes and appear as a touring bus like the rock stars have – complete with bunk beds and kitchenette. Without a prospective hotel available, the ship would house the committee members comfortably.

"You are most welcome, Rey. I'm sorry Mr. Hardgold doesn't have a hotel in Alaska; but if your next destination contains a hotel, I will arrange your accommodations. Have a safe trip," Frankle replied. "If I hear any news regarding someone looking for Tony, I will let you know so you can bring him back. We don't want anyone thinking you have kidnapped him, but I think he will enjoy traveling with you. I know he is really excited."

"It was great to meet you, Frank." Vedagy said.

"Yes, thank you," several committee members agreed at the same time.

"I'll call you in a few days, Cousin. Take care and thank you for coming through with the digs," Frinkle said as he gave Frankle a hug.

"You're sounding more human every day, Frinkle," Frankle laughed. "Go have fun. Let me know how things are going. I have a vested interest in your final decision, ya know."

Everyone said goodbye as they boarded the ship. Tony was really excited that he was chosen to join the committee on their mission. Hopefully, they would find Santa and he would allow Tony to become one of his elves. He couldn't wait!

## Profile – Frankle

Name: Frankle (fran-kuhl)
Nickname: Frank
Planet: Pluto (plew-toh)
Galaxy: Milky Way (mil-kee way)
Specialty: Lives on Earth
Dietary Needs: no restrictions
Other:

- » Cousin to Frinkle
- » Works for a millionaire who owns a chain of hotels
- » Caused the first hole in the ozone layer upon entering Earth's atmosphere
- » Immigrated to Earth when Pluto was no longer deemed a planet

# Beeb's Second Report

Galactic Day 2 –

*This has been a busy day. We landed on the rooftop of Surtic Hotel in New York, New York, in the United States of America on planet Earth of the Milky Way Galaxy at T minus 1008 hours. Frankle, Frinkle's cousin, met us at the landing and introduced us to something called a parade. It had flying balloons – much bigger than the ones made on my planet. Many humans gathered on the avenue to watch these balloons and other humans pass by – it seemed to please all who participated as well as the spectators.*

*The crystals seem to be working because we were not detected as being from another galaxy. We mingled with the humans on the avenue after viewing our quarters. They are called people and seemed to be quite happy. One female gave President Reyclebin a piece of cloth called a blanket to aid his comfort, but the temperature and the* gravity proved too much for him. He froze solid due to his high water content – in spite of the suit specially designed for us. The others showed no signs of freezing. President Reyclebin was taken to the ship where he has been monitoring the mission and assessing our progress.

Vedagy, Morach, and Portamer brought back a stray when they returned from the market. His name is Tony and appears to be approximately one and one-third galactic years. He is full of energy and very knowledgeable about someone called Santa Claus. This Santa Claus person is reputed to inspire happiness in people all over Earth. We have begun a search for this Santa Claus but have not located him as yet.

The people in this region seem content. There are some faces that appear humble, resigned, or sad, but many seem content – even happy. We have not seen anything resembling the negative pictures shown during the council meeting as a result of the scouting party's research. Morach seems both pleased and dejected. I believe he wants to find the source of the satellite transmissions to release his self-inflicted guilt.

Clombic carries minimal weapons so as not to incite violence among the humans if none is forthcoming, but she keeps her taser and field knife ready if trouble should arise. Portamer reminds us what happiness is and keeps us in check if we get over zealous. He has proven to be the stabilizer of emotions that are easy for us to mimic here on Earth.

Frinkle is Frinkle. He is young and has taken to Earth life well. Limdon and Pumbint monitor the ship's operation, as well as our coms units, in case we have problems in Earth's atmosphere.

I have been observing all aspects of our mission and will continue my reports at the end of each galactic day. We leave in a few minutes for our next destination.

This concludes my report for galactic day two on the mission to Search for Happiness and Assess the Destiny of Earth (S.H.A.D.E.).

# *Profile – Reyclebin*

Name:  Reyclebin (ray-kluh-bin)
Nickname:  Rey
Planet:  Bolcus (bowl-cus)
Galaxy:  Buffinger (buff-een-jer)
Specialty:  Leadership
Dietary Needs:  Liquid
Other:
>  » President of the Universal Council
> of Galaxies
>  » Chairman of S.H.A.D.E.
>  » Married (no children)

## five

## North Pole

Because of the darkness, the ship was able to get within fifteen miles of North Pole without being detected. The captain pressed a few buttons, twisted a few crystals, and the ship was transformed into a touring bus. This was how the people of North Pole first met the committee. As they rolled into town, citizens were looking out their windows to see what famous person could be coming to visit. They were used to celebrities coming to town to see Santa and it was Christmas every day in North Pole. The lamp posts were decorated with candy canes and the streets were named after Christmas icons such as Snowman Lane, St. Nicholas Drive, and Kris Kringle Drive to name a few.

The captain followed the signs to Santa Claus' house located on Santa Claus Lane. A big Santa statue stood outside his house. But, what's this? A sign on the front of the house said it's a gift shop!  Everyone on the bus saw the sign at the same time.

Tony let out a cry, "Nooooo!  It can't be! Santa lives at the north pole!"

"Tony, we will find him.  Let's find a place to park for the night and we will get some answers in the morning," Reyclebin suggested.  "We will get some rest and ask the residents about the whereabouts of Santa."

Everyone was disappointed, but agreed to get some rest then mingle with the locals in the morning.  The other downside was not knowing when the morning appeared.  The sun shone only five and one-half hours each day.  On the shortest day of the year, December 21st, the sun shone for less than four hours.  The captain parked near Ice Park, which contained ice sculptures of Christmas trees, cabins, Santa, angels, and a nativity scene.  It was a nice view and perked up the spirits of the committee just a little bit.

They finally fell into a fitful sleep but woke only five hours later when they heard commotion outside.  People had started going into Santa's house or, rather, gift shop.  The time had come for them to go out into the freezing cold to find some answers. Reyclebin stayed behind due to the freezing cold; while the rest of the team made sure they were wearing their crystals and filed out of the bus.

The people going into the gift shop stopped and stared. Seeing the ten people dressed in jumpsuits of various colors was a bit auspicious. It looked like a special government agency was descending upon them. *What agency are they from? Why are they here?* They would find out soon enough because the group was heading into the gift shop wearing serious expressions.

"Hello," Tony said. "Does Santa live here? It says this is Santa's house, but it says – and looks like – it's a gift shop."

"Oh, I am sorry, young man," said the shopkeeper. "This is just the gateway to the real north pole, but... ummm... Santa moved his workshop."

"What?! Where did he move to? How do we get there?" Tony asked with fear and horror in his voice.

Vedagy put her arm around Tony as she said, "Sir, we came all the way from New York to see Santa. Can you help us?"

"My, my, that's a long way. Well, Santa decided that too many people had found his secret workshop, so it was no longer a secret. People kept coming, though, so we designed this town to draw the people away from his workshop. Unfortunately, some people still persisted and put it on television – which only took time away from what Santa does best: build toys to make children happy."

"That's terrible!" Morach chimed in. He remembered seeing something about the north pole secret being exposed on the satellites. That was part of the negativity in his study. His interest was piqued now.

"Yes it is," the shopkeeper continued. "That's why he moved his workshop. But, he hasn't told anyone where it is."

"Do you have any ideas? We have to find him!" Tony pleaded.

"The only thing I can tell you is that he is originally from Holland, I think. I know the legends say the first Santa was a Dutchman. That might be a good place to look. I'm sorry I can't tell you anything more. You might try to write him a letter, though," he encouraged.

"If I write a letter, it will go to the north pole and he isn't there." Tony said sadly.

"Thank you for your time," Clombic said. "We'll be going now."

"Could I get this statue of Santa, please?" Limdon asked. "I'd like to show our chairman who it is we are looking for. He's a little under the weather and confined to the bus."

"Oh, I'm so sorry to hear that. Is he the reason you are looking for Santa? Is it like a special wish or something? I get it. You're from the Make-a-Wish Foundation! Yes, you most certainly may have the     figurine – no charge. Let me wrap it for you."

The shopkeeper had his assistant wrap the figurine and smiled at the group as they left. He was radiating happiness with his thoughts that he had some small part in helping some-one get their last wish. He only wished he could have done more.

Snickering, the group entered the bus. "Limdon, you didn't even try to correct him when he thought we were from that founda-tion," Pumbint chastised.

"He seemed so happy, though, when he thought he was helping someone," Vedagy said.

"Yes, he did, didn't he," Limdon added with a smile. Noticing Tony sulking in the corner, she went over to cheer him up. "Tony, I know it's disappointing that we didn't find

Santa here, but we will. It may take a few days, but we'll find him."

"Thanks, Lim. Can we go to Holland next?" Tony asked.

"We need to speak to Rey first. He makes the final decisions, but I'm sure we will get there soon," Limdon assured him.

"Limmy, Pumbint, can we speak with you for a moment?" the captain motioned to Reyclebin as he asked. "In here." The captain led them to the crystals control room. "Sir?"

"Go ahead, Captain," Reyclebin permitted.

"We have a situation. We used a lot of power flying over here and transforming the ship. Normally, we can recharge with the sunlight and, sometimes, moonlight. However, there is very little daylight in this area of the Earth and... one of the receptacles was damaged during the change-over."

"How much power would you say we have left, Captain?" Pumbint asked.

"Well, we can transform again if we want to risk losing another receptacle, or we can travel south to where the sun shines longer to build the power and make repairs. It's your call, Sir," the captain nodded to Reyclebin as he finished his assessment.

"Can you two repair the damage?" Reyclebin asked.

"I'd like to go south to get more sunlight to work in. It would help to charge the crystals at the same time we assess the extent of the damage, Sir," Limdon replied.

"I agree, Sir, the more we can charge the crystals the better able we will be to repair the damage," Pumbint added.

"Very well. We will travel south and do the repairs before we continue on our mission," Reyclebin announced. "We will leave as soon as the sun rises to give us a little extra power."

"I will begin making the arrangements," the captain said.

While the captain planned a route southward, Limdon and Pumbint took a survey of their supplies and started a list of what they needed to make the repairs... solar panel, sticky tape, weather stripping, etc. They had basic tools, but their spare solar power receptacle had not survived the entrance through the ozone layer and the shape change. Lucky for the crew, the inventors were onboard and one of them had sold a flawless sapphire for

half of a million dollars. The cost of the repairs would not be a factor.

Reyclebin gave a watered-down version of
the situation to the rest of the group. He gave
them some money for food and sent them to
the neighborhood 24-hour grocery store to
stock up on staples. Vedagy had her list
ready, too. The bus was equipped with a
kitchen; but it had limited space, which made
it hard to make more than a couple dishes at
one time. To unite the tastes of the different
galaxies, Vedagy had to make sure she had
something for everyone in as few choices as
possible – meat for the carnivores, vegetables
for the herbivores, and sugar for Portamer.
Most humans eat a little of all categories in
each meal, but these weren't humans – except
Tony.

The sun was just beginning to rise when
the group returned with arms full of grocery
bags. They had enough food to feed them all
for at least a week. The repairs should be
done well before then so the bus could transform into their ship again and they could
continue to Holland. Until then, they would
have to be content with their small living area.
Finding storage for all the food proved chal-

lenging, but it was finally stored and the sun was still shining.

"We have about three hours of sunlight if we stay here, so we need to get going. The power is sufficient to keep us mobile for at least eight hours with continued sunshine," the captain told Limdon.

"Thank you, Captain. I will make sure everyone is ready to be underway," she replied. Returning to the living area of the bus, Limdon asked that everyone be seated while the captain negotiated the roads. Travel became a little rough compared to the smooth flying they were used to before now. Not all roads were freshly paved and smooth, either, especially in the wild parts of Alaska: the area they were trying to vacate as quickly as possible.

# Profile –Frinkle

Name:  Frinkle (freen-kuhl)
Nickname:  Frinkle
Planet:  Pluto (no longer a planet)
Galaxy:  Milky Way (mil-kee way)
Specialty:  Cousin to Earth citizen
Dietary Needs:  no restrictions
Other:

» Can telepathically communicate
with his cousin, Frankle, who
immigrated to Earth

six

## *Seattle*

It was raining so hard the captain could barely see out the windshield. He found the next off-ramp and exited the I-5 interstate at a city named Seattle. They were somewhere in the northwestern corner of the United States – according to the map on the screen in front of him. He hoped they would stay here for a couple days so he could rest. He'd been doing all the driving and it was sometimes treacherous with holes, rocks, mud, snow, and ice until they reached the paved roads – even they had ice, snow, and holes. Although the team had stopped at roadside stations for brief periods of rest and food, the captain needed some solid sleep.

Limdon and Pumbint were worried that the power reserve would be getting low if they didn't get some sun soon. The sky was filled

with dark clouds and rain, which was hiding the rejuvenating sunlight. They had opted not to transform the bus back into the ship until they could repair the solar panels, but they were using the reserve power faster than expected. They had approximately three days of power left if they continued using it at this rate. Maybe Seattle would have some of the supplies they needed.

Tony and Frinkle were getting cabin fever from being cooped up for the past three days. They needed to get out and exercise as all young boys do. The energy emanating from them could have powered the bus if they could only figure out how to harness it. Reyclebin was trying to come up with a task to keep the boys busy when Vedagy suggested they help her make meat loaf. Relief and gratitude were evident in Reyclebin's expression.

Although meat loaf may sound like an easy meal to make, Vedagy had a special recipe and technique that would keep the boys occupied for a bit. She combined ground turkey and ground beef in a large bowl. She had Tony chop onions in a chopper and had Frinkle grind toasted bread in the food processor – both were safe as long as they didn't take the lids off. While they were doing their jobs, Vedagy chopped the fresh herbs: cilantro, thyme, oregano, dill, marjoram, rosemary, and chives. They added their ingredients to the meat mixture.

The boys (after washing their hands for the third time in the past hour) stuck their clean hands into the meat and squished it through their fingers with happy giggles. The goal was to mix the herbs, onions, and bread crumbs thoroughly into the meat. After a few minutes, Vedagy added a few raw chicken eggs, some Worcestershire sauce, ketchup, mustard, and a little sour cream. Tony and Frinkle were laughing and imitating animal sounds while they worked. This was a great idea.

"Okay, boys," Vedagy began, "it looks mixed enough now. You did a great job! We aren't done yet, but you can wash your hands... yes, again," she added as she tousled Tony's hair when he started to protest. "Then we can put them into pans before we make the potatoes." They all washed their hands and Vedagy drained the potatoes she had boiling so they could cool while they filled the pans with meat.

They divided the meat into three sections and formed them into cylindrical loaves to fit the loaf pans. They wanted them rounded so the mashed potatoes could be packed down the sides and over the top. Mashing the potatoes was fun, too. The boys each got a masher and used their energy to make the whole potatoes resemble mush. Vedagy had to stop them before the potatoes became liquefied. She added some mayonnaise, sour cream, dill, and lemon to the potatoes and mixed them together. She then let the boys spoon some of the potatoes over the meat loaves and wrote their names on top of the loaves with ketchup. When the loaves were assembled, Vedagy put them in the oven that was preheated to 350 degrees and set the timer for 45 minutes.

The clock said it was mid-day, but the sky was dark and wet. If it grew any colder, the rain would change to snow. Snow would bring its own set of problems; but with rain, Beeb would be confined to the ship until it stopped. With his sponge-like body, he would be swollen for days and that wouldn't do his reporting any good - dripping on everything he wrote. He would just take this time to work on his reports.

Portamer, Morach, and Clombic (with her ever-present taser and field knife) went on a scouting mission. They were looking for the hardware and building supplies stores for Limdon and Pumbint. Actually, that was the excuse they used to get out of the bus for a few hours. They preferred to take a walk in the rain rather than stay cooped up any longer. They watched some people hurrying from doorway to doorway to escape the falling drops of water. Others were resigned to the rain and some even seemed to embrace it.

The street lamps were alternately adorned with large colorful wreaths and blue-tinted snowflakes. The shop windows were outlined with garland strands in different colors and designs. One was purple with red twisting through it; another was green with little white lights; and yet another was red and white striped with little cutouts of candy canes hanging from it. Some windows even had wintery scenes set up along the inside window ledges.

The hardware store caught the group's attention as they approached. The window display held a life-sized Santa sitting at a workbench, frozen in the act of hammering the final wooden peg into a toy hobby horse, while a variety of wood-working tools lay within reach. Electric candles provided the lighting for his work.

A little silver bell jingled above their heads as the three entered the store. The scent of cinnamon wax mingled with the pungent smells of the oils used to treat the tools against rust. The store had an old-time feel like the reputed mom-and-pop stores from the horse-and-buggy days. However, Portamer, Clombic, and Morach just saw a bunch of gadgets cluttered about the shelves. They didn't see anything resembling the solar panels on the ship, so they decided to ask someone.

"Excuse me," Clombic called to an employee as he walked toward them. "Do you have any sun energy receptors?"

"I'm sorry," answered the clerk, "what exactly are you looking for?"

"We seek a receptacle for solar energy," Portamer replied.

"Do you mean solar panels?" the clerk asked with a puzzled look.

"Yes, that is the term – solar panels," Portamer confirmed.

"You're kidding, right?" Seeing the stoic looks on the faces before him, the clerk determined they were not, in fact, kidding and began laughing. "Hey, Hal. These yo-yos are looking for solar panels!" he called to another employee.

"Yeah, right! Like we would have such a thing in *this* town!" the other clerk shouted back. "We have clouds over 200 days a year – solar panels would be useless most of the time!"

"You are very helpful. Thank you for your time," Morach interjected.

Amidst the clerks' continued laughter, the three out-of-towners left the store. The jingle from the bell above the door added a final mocking note. Disheartened, they made their way back to the ship to warm up and dry off. Several people greeted them with smiles along the way, but the rudeness of the sales clerks was still fresh in their minds and the smiles were not returned.

As they boarded the bus, Vedagy called them to dinner. For appetizers, she offered a choice of beef and barley soup or a green salad topped with three types of legumes: pinto beans, white beans, and kidney beans. A sweet-potato pie had been purchased just for Portamer, providing the sugar he needed as well as a little nutrition. The main course consisted of the meatloaf the boys had made; green-bean casserole; and a fruit tray with a sweet, cream-cheese dipping sauce. Dessert was to be a chocolate mousse, but Beeb and Portamer practically drank it down, so there was none left for anyone else. Portamer, in a rare moment of good will, shared his sweet-potato pie with everyone since he had devoured the mousse.

Everyone's tastes were accommodated: Vedagy preferred vegetarian; Portamer lived on sugar; Limdon and Pumbint preferred meat and vegetables, but didn't eat sugar; Reyclebin preferred water and liquid nutrition such as soups; Beeb had a weakness for chocolate (it acted like alcohol for him); Clombic was a carnivore who rarely ate vegetables; and the rest pretty much ate anything laid before them. The variety could create a challenge for Vedagy, but most of the time everyone fended for themselves.

During dinner, Portamer, Morach, and

Clombic related their experience in town. They described the decorations along the streets and in the store-front windows. When they recounted the part about the hardware store clerks, they had a touch of anger in their voices.

"The first clerk was very rude and laughed at us when Portamer explained what we were looking for," commented Clombic.

"But then he yelled to his friend and told him what we wanted. They were both howling before we could leave the store," Morach added despondently.

The most important point Limdon, Pumbint, and Reyclebin heard was that solar panels were not available here because of the exorbitant amount of clouds and rain. Limdon started wondering, *How long will the power last if we stay here any longer? Will we find replacement panels? Even if we don't find replacements, we need to recharge. Where do we have to go to get sunlight?* She was concerned; but didn't want to alarm the others, so she sat quietly.

The only thing Pumbint could think was... *What are we going to do if we don't get the parts? We can't make it back home if we don't have fully charged and operating solar power receptacles. I'm* not giving up yet, we've been on Earth less than two weeks and if we have to spend the rest of the time finding something that will work (or building them ourselves), we will.

Reyclebin was worried about the captain. Being confined to the ship had increased the friendship and bond between the two. *Even though the captain is sleeping now,* Reyclebin pondered, *will it be enough rest for him to continue driving? Maybe one of the others could drive for a while, but whom? Vedagy and I are too short; Beeb doesn't have the reach; Limdon and Pumbint need to save their strength to repair the ship when we get the proper equipment; Morach is too big; Clombic is too tall; Frinkle is too easily distracted... that just leaves Portamer. I'll ask him after dinner,* Reyclebin thought.

## seven

## Traveling South

Portamer could understand why the captain had become so exhausted while driving. There wasn't anything mentally stimulating about sitting in a virtual parking lot called the interstate highway. They would move forward slowly for a few minutes then they would sit still for another few minutes. There should be something they could do to break this up.

Beeb told him that he picked up a partial conversation with his telepathic skills. Apparently, a semi-truck had jackknifed and overturned across both of the southbound lanes. The authorities were redirecting traffic to Highway 101 along the Pacific coastline. He didn't get any more information than that before he lost concentration. Beeb had confessed to Portamer that this was the first time he had really tried to use telepathy across a distance and it took a lot of energy.

*Finally.* Portamer thought as the traffic started to move a little quicker. Some of the cars had been directed across the median and were going around the truck. (Alas, only the cars that couldn't be directed off the interstate – because they were past the final exit – were able to go around the accident.) Everyone else was moving to the other highway or finding other shortcuts. Because the locals, who were familiar with the area, were finding alternate avenues or waiting in town for the road to clear, Portamer was moving quickly and making progress.

Fortunately, the sun had been shining for most of the day, so the reserves had been able to recharge a little bit. *Un*fortunately, they had been stuck in that traffic jam, so they didn't make much progress. They were all hopeful that the sun would shine again tomorrow and allow the solar panel receptors to fully charge. Even with one not functioning, the ones that remained could power them for a few more days.

The sun was setting when they finally made it to Highway 101. They continued traveling through half the night so they could get ahead of the rest of the traffic, then found a parking area near the beach to eat and rest.

When they awoke, they realized they were moving. The captain was back at the wheel after getting a full day and night's rest. He was quite refreshed and knew that the parking area they had stopped at last night would not have the supplies needed to repair the ship. He wanted it repaired as soon as possible because he was tired of the slow pace of getting from one point to another.

Tony and Frinkle were getting restless again and Pumbint and Limdon were getting anxious. Reyclebin suggested they stop at the next town to let the boys run and to find out the most likely place to find the solar panels they needed.

"Sir," Portamer began, "would it be prudent to contact Frankle to query where we may find the panels? His employer does have hotels around the world. I would suspect he has them in the most prominent areas."

"Of course, Portamer! What a brilliant idea!" Reyclebin exclaimed. "Frinkle. Come over here, please," he continued.

"Yes, Sir?"

"Do you have a way to contact Frankle?"

"Of course, Sir. We can sense each other telepathically when we want. What is it you need to know?" Frinkle asked.

"We need you to contact Frank and ask him where Mr. Hardgold has hotels," Reyclebin replied. He then relayed Portamer's idea.

"Awesome idea, Port. I'll get right on it." Frankle immediately set about trying to contact his cousin in New York.

*Frank. Frank, are you there?*

*Frinkle? Is that you? How have you been?*

*I'm fine, Cousin. We have a slight problem and were hoping you could help us.*

*Oh my! I'll do whatever I can. Is everyone okay?* Frankle asked, alarmed and concerned.

*Everyone is fine, Frank. We had a little technical difficulty. One of our solar panels broke during our last transformation and we need a replacement. We've traveled by land for the past few days and have not found anywhere that sells them.*

*That's terrible! How can I help? I'm not too familiar with solar panels and the sort.* Frankle responded.

*I understand, Frank. What we need is to know where Mr. Hardgold has hotels. We're thinking that the cities he has them in would be large enough to sell the parts we need.*

*That's brilliant! Let's see. Where are you now?*

*Just a moment. I'll find out.* "Captain, where are we located?" Frinkle asked.

"The last sign I saw said Coos Bay is just ahead. I think we are in Oregon."

"Thanks." *Frank?*

*Yeah, I'm here.*

*We are near Coos Bay in Oregon. Does that help?*

*Yeah, but I don't recall any hotels in Oregon. I'll have to look at a map and get back to you. I think there is one in California – which is south of you. Just keep going south until I get back to you.*

*Thanks, Frank. You're the best!*

Frinkle relayed the conversation to Reyclebin and Portamer. Reyclebin decided they should drive a couple more hours, then take a break to enjoy some of the surroundings and mingle with the people. After all, their mission was to find signs of happiness on Earth.

# Profile – Limdon

Name:  Limdon (lim-dun)
Nickname:  Lim, Limmy
Planet:  Conog (coh-nog)
Galaxy:  Hoxtil (hawks-tull)
Specialty:  Master of Crystal Energy
Dietary Needs:
> » Meat & vegetables – no sugar

Other:
> » Knows the energy properties of
>   every crystal and how best to use
>   their energy
> » Designed the disguise unit to inte-
>   grate with the coms unit
> » Favorite color is pink

## Beeb's Third Report

Galactic Day 3 -

*This day has been wrought with dismay and revelation. We arrived at North Pole, Alaska, in the United States of America at T minus 840 hours in search of Santa Claus. The residents of this region were sad when they admitted Santa Claus does not live where humans all over Earth believe he lives. He has moved his operation – possibly to a place called Holland.*

*We had some minor malfunctions with the ship when it was transformed into a double-decker touring bus. One of the solar energy receptors was damaged and our power was limited, so we had to travel by land to a place where Limdon and Pumbint could find replacement panels (the spare was also broken during transformation.) Our first attempt was in Seattle, Washington, in the United States of America.*

This area was full of gloom due to the constant precipitation called rain. I was forced to remain onboard due to my presumed absorption of said rain. Portamer, Morach, and Clombic scouted for the supplies needed but were unsuccessful in locating anyplace that carried them. The people appeared joyful when asked about the solar panels. They suggested we continue south because there is not sufficient sunshine in this area to warrant their use.

We are running out of power because we are not getting enough sunshine to replenish the solar panels – which cleanse and recharge the crystals. The general attitude onboard is somber. We continued southward in hopes of finding sunshine and supplies.

There was an accident on the main interstate road so we were redirected to a smaller highway along the coastline. While this road was less maintained, it had nice scenery. We did have some sunshine to charge our receptacles, but the energy was used quickly due to the increased travel time. Alas, the bit of sunshine we managed to get between the highways was replaced by clouds once we arrived at the coast –  causing us to use the reserves even faster.

Portamer suggested we contact Frankle (Frinkle's cousin in New York City) to determine where Mr. Hardgold (Frankle's employer) has his hotels. The thought process was that the larger cities worthy of his hotels would also have a hardware or specialty store large enough to supply the panels. Frankle told us San Francisco and Hollywood were the only cities on the West Coast that housed the   hotels.

On our way south, we stopped to rest and visited an animal park in Oregon. It was interesting to see so many animals from Earth gathered in one place for everyone to visit. There was a group of school children learning about the animals, so we joined them.

The park housed raccoons, also known as bandits because they have a tendency to pick pockets; elk, which Tony said were like reindeer except the antlers on reindeer are fuzzier;  and rabbits, furry little creatures with long ears and wiggly noses that hop from place to place. (It is purported that rabbits deliver Easter baskets filled with candy and gifts to children every year – like Santa does at Christmas, but in a different way.) There were other animals, too, called lions, monkeys, tigers, bears, peacock, and a lynx that resembled Limdon. There were lots more animals and it gave us a good education about the different species and inhabitants of Earth.     After our visit to the park, it was agreed we would try San    Francisco,

*California, as it was closest. Again, I stayed onboard due to the vast amount of moisture in the air (called fog).*

*This fog made it difficult to see very far at a time. However, the sun appeared for a few hours and we are almost at full charge again – minus the broken receptacles. Replacement supplies are not forth-coming, unfortunately, but Frankle did some additional research and found a place in Hollywood that will have our supplies. We are traveling there now and should arrive soon. We hope to have full repairs and power in a few galactic hours. Spirits are beginning to pick up as we get closer.*

*This concludes my report for galactic day three on the mission to find happiness on Earth.*

## eight

## Hollywood, CA

After searching in every coastal town they came to for the necessary parts to make their repairs, they finally arrived in Hollywood, CA. This was where they were told to look when they stopped in San Francisco. Now they had to look for Magnolia Boulevard and watch for a big sun on top of a building. That would be the place to get the rest of the supplies they needed. Everyone was getting excited!

While they were en route to the right street, Tony spotted a few stores advertising Santa's visiting hours. He knew these were just Santa's helpers, but suggested they stop and visit a couple of the stores anyway.

They walked into a large mall and saw smiling faces everywhere. Portamer, who is the skeptic of the bunch, was beginning to see that there were some places where people were happier than in others. Then he saw a woman holding a piece of paper, looking at a monitor, and crying.

He walked up to her and asked if she was sad. She said, "No. I am very happy."

"Why are you crying then?" Portamer inquired.

"Because I just won $100,000," she said in disbelief. "I needed the money to pay for my little girl's operation and now I have it."

"In that case, I am happy for you," Portamer decided and walked away. When he returned to the group, he looked perplexed.

"What is the matter, Portamer?" Frinkle asked. "You look different."

"I am reflecting on my conversation with the young woman across the way," he began. "She was crying, but she said she was happy. That is an odd way of showing it."

"People show they are happy in lots of ways, Portamer," Tony added. "Some laugh, some cry, some smile, some spend money, some give things away, and some don't show it at all. You can't always tell just by looking at someone if they are happy or not. Is that what's been bothering you? You think nobody is happy if they aren't smiling and laughing? You don't laugh, either. Are you happy?"

"You are very intuitive, young Tony. I am indeed happy – though I may not show it as you have described. Perhaps I should look more closely at people than just what is on the outside." He pondered that for a few seconds and said, "Yes, I do believe I must look at this from another angle. Thank you, Tony. As much as I don't like to admit it, you have given me a new perspective to consider."

"Good. Now that we cleared that up, let's see about getting those parts we need," Pumbint said and led the way back to the bus.

Morach was also doing some thinking after speaking with a few of the humans in the mall. He was told that, if he wanted to find Santa, he should go to Universal Studios where he would most likely find many Santas to interview. He may even find the real one mixed in. It has happened before. He had purchased a map of Hollywood just before leaving the mall. He studied it now to see the distance between Universal Studios and Magnolia Boulevard, which was their current destination.

Pumbint, Limdon, and Reyclebin (who

was able to leave the ship now that they were in a warmer climate) went to the supply store together. They found all the parts necessary to complete the repairs and improve the trans- forming system. Now they just needed a place to perform the work.

When they returned to the bus, Morach was talking to the captain about the park he found only a few miles away. Reyclebin, Limdon, and Pumbint agreed that, since that part of the park was open to camping, it would be the perfect place to settle for the two Earth days it would take to do the repairs. It was beginning to get dark, so they decided to stop for groceries then get some rest after dinner. They would begin work in the morn- ing.

Morach was beside himself with anticipa- tion. He wasn't sure what he would find, but he knew he had to try. Of course, Morach hadn't mentioned that Universal City was just a short hike from the park. He began making a mental list of things to ask the Santas when he got to the studios, and he wondered how many Santas he would find.

\* \* \* \* \*

The sun was shining brightly when Tony awoke to the sound of parts being removed from the storage bins under the bus. Catching the aroma of Vedagy's cooking as it wafted past his nose, he was up and dressed in one minute flat. After all, who could resist Vedagy's cooking? She made her special biscuits and gravy; wheat pancakes with homemade wild berry syrup; vegetable omelets for the vegetarians (that would be Vedagy) and anyone else who wanted them; sausage patties and bacon; and to top it off, she made a chocolate cake and was serving it with whipped cream and cherries! Oh my! What a feast! It looked like she had also started preparing dishes for lunch and dinner so she wouldn't have to cook or be in the way during the repairs. Smart idea she had. For such a short alien, she had a lot of tall ambition.

With such a beautiful day beginning, they unanimously agreed to eat at the picnic tables outside. Nobody noticed that Morach had quietly left the group after finishing his breakfast and putting an apple and biscuit wrapped in a napkin into his knapsack. He almost forgot his bottle of water, but remembered before he left. Easily away, he began his short hike to Universal City and the studios within. Whistling a tune he didn't recognize (he must have picked it up from one of the locals), he cut across the fields in the shortest line. Others had done the same, it seemed, because there was a path trampled in the tall grass as if many feet had passed this way.

*Just look at all those cars going through the gate! And they all appear to have Santas in them!* Morach thought with excitement. He was getting closer to the place he was certain could tell him more about the negative transmissions they intercepted. *The fate of this planet depends on my finding more information. That must be the entrance to the city and the studios. I need to follow them. Ok, so how am I going to get in? This is a fine idea! I've got it!*

"Excuse me, Sir," Morach began as he stepped onto the passenger-side running board of an RV in line. "Can I ask you a few questions?" He was thankful he had found a clip board at the same store he purchased the map. This made it look plausible that he was asking questions.

"Sure, Chap, climb on in and let's chat a spell. Looks like we'll be a few minutes going through the gate," he drawled with a slightly southern accent. "What can I help you with, young feller?"

Morach was amazed at how easy it was to talk to this kind, older human with his rose-colored cheeks and round face. His white hair was barely visible beneath his crimson and white cap; but his bushy, white eyebrows left no mystery that his hair was just as thick and white. His long, soft beard hid the lower half of his face but his rosy nose and lips fit just perfectly with his cheeks. He was a postcard-perfect Santa! "Forgive me, kind Sir," Morach stuttered. "You look like the pictures I've seen and nobody has ever fit the description of Santa as well as you do. I'm just in awe of the kindness I can feel radiate from you."

"Well, to tell you a secret, I've been told that a time or two. Maybe it's because I am the real Santa? It's okay, Morach, you don't need to be alarmed. I expected you and wanted to help you on your quest for knowledge. We don't have to tell anyone that I'm the real Santa just yet."

"Oh... Oh... Okay. I'm so nervous! I didn't expect to meet the real Santa on my first try! Hey, how did you know my name? Why did you expect me? And how do you know of my quest for knowledge? Do you know what it is I'm looking for? I'm not even sure *I* know what I'm looking for."

"I am Santa Claus. I know who has been naughty and nice, who has been good or bad, and who is happy or sad. I..."

"What?!" Morach exclaimed. "You know who is happy and sad?! Oh my goodness! You need to talk to the rest of the committee! They need to hear this! Are there a lot of happy people? If so, why did our systems pick up negative transmissions from your satellites? How can we prove that people are happy?"

"Morach, my son," Santa began, "Part of the reason you are here today is to learn what signals you have been intercepting and what those signals represent. If you can turn off your disguise crystal for a bit, I can introduce you as my elf. You are in the perfect place to be seen as yourself and not be thought alien to Earth. Hurry, now, we are almost to the gate."

Morach turned off his disguise crystal to reveal his true form. His body was covered in short blue hair that wasn't quite thick enough to be fur; and his hands and feet were orange.

A single green eye sat in the center of the raised bump on the top of his head.  His button nose was incongruent with his large chin and barely-noticeable ears.  Now that the crystal had been turned off, Santa could see how cramped Morach was in the passenger seat.

Because of his wrestler-sized bulk, Morach was hunched over – yet his head was still against the roof of the cab.

## *Profile – Morach*

Name:  Morach (mor-ock)
Nickname:  Mark
Planet:  Tivar (tee-var)
Galaxy:  Kakit (kaa-kit)
Specialty:  Intergalactic Studies
Dietary Needs:  no restrictions
Other:

> » Intercepted the negative transmissions that led to a decision to destroy Earth
>
> » Advocated to give Earth a second chance by looking for happiness first hand
>
> » Looking for explanation of negative transmissions

## nine

## Morach's Movie

"Name please," the gate guard stated, sounding quite bored with his job.

"Santa Claus"

"Right. For what movie are you auditioning?"

"Santa Unites the Worlds," Santa replied.

"Who's that with you – an alien elf?" he chuckled. At Santa's smile, he asked, "What's his name?"

"Mark"

"Last name?"

"Mark Morach. Cruel, I know. We just call him Morach."

"Auditioning for the same movie, Morach?"

"Yes, Sir," Morach answered quietly.

"Take the first left, go two trailers and turn right. You'll see the line of Santas and aliens. That's where you'll audition. Here are your packets and audition numbers. The forms need to be completed before your numbers are called. Trust me. You'll have plenty of time to fill them out."

"Thank you, Dan," Santa said, reading the man's nametag. "A very Merry Christmas to you."

"You're the first to wish me a Merry Christmas all day. Good luck to both of you," he said with a smile.

With a nod, Santa began inching forward to follow the directions given by Dan.

* * * * *

"333 and 334 please report to the audition trailer."

"Numbers three-hundred-thirty-three and three-hundred-thirty-four! Santa and Moron!" The loud speaker screeched their numbers and names when the person speaking didn't see any immediate movement. A shared giggle arose from the crowd as the names were announced.

"Oh, they are calling our numbers, Morach, let's go." Santa smiled at Morach as he took the alien's hand in his and led him to the audition trailer. "Don't be nervous; you will do fine. This is just the first step to getting the answers you need."

*****

Meanwhile, back at the park, Limdon and Pumbint had begun the repairs. Portamer was pondering his new information and Vedagy was playing catch with Tony and Frinkle – using an orange as they didn't have a ball. They opted against batting it to preserve the "ball" for continued play.

Clombic was assisting Pumbint with some of the higher points while Pader, the captain, watched with interest. Reyclebin was taking a nap and Beeb was working on his next report. Everyone was busy and didn't notice Morach was missing until…

"Rey, Sir. I-I-I mean Rey. I'm sorry to disturb you, but we can't locate Mark. We decided to take a lunch break and were gathering everyone together – by the way, lunch is ready – but nobody has seen Mark since this morning. Should we go looking for him?" Frinkle asked the sleep-dazed leader.

"Have you checked the entire ship and the park?" Reyclebin asked.

"Yes, Sir. We even walked down to the pond in case he had fallen asleep under a shady tree; but he isn't anywhere." Worried and unsure of the reaction he would get upon telling Reyclebin the next bit of news, he bolstered his courage and blurted, "Portamer found a map of the area and there's a movie studio about half a mile away and some of us think maybe he went there because he still wants to prove he isn't crazy about the negative signals that he intercepted and that there must be some reason he got those signals and they may have been false readings and people on Earth really are happy in their own way." Panting from the rushed speech and lack of breath, Frinkle again held his breath while waiting for Reyclebin's reaction.

"Well, Frinkle," he began. "It seems you know what has been bothering Morach since we left. I knew there was something, but he wouldn't confide in me. Thank you for letting me know. Breathe, lad. Now that I know and Portamer has found a map, let's discuss the situation while we eat. If Morach truly has gone to the movie studio, he won't be back for lunch." Pausing to turn on his disguise, he followed Frinkle out to the picnic table where lunch was laid out.

*****

"Okay, kid," the director called, "remember to get those arms up when you attack. Places everyone... rolling... aaand... action!"

Santa hadn't noticed his elves had turned into little monsters as they were loading the sleigh, so when Morach jumped up from under the sacks already loaded, Santa was stunned. Morach came at him with a fierce growl – his arms outstretched – as he wrapped his long orange fingers around Santa's beard and pulled him off balance. The other monster elves were pushing him into the back of the sleigh and started tying his hands and feet.

Although Santa was speechless for a moment, he began noticing the eyes of the monster elves. Every elf's eyes were vacant and trance-like. "What is going on here?" he finally managed to ask. "What happened to you?"

In response, the elves looked at him with their blank eyes and cocked their heads to one side as if they were listening to something. Just as quickly, they went back to their tasks. Some were unloading the sleigh while others were still trying to tie up Santa's feet – they were having trouble with the knots because Santa kept moving his feet. Morach still had hold of Santa's beard and was holding him still while he was being tied up.

"That's it!" Santa exclaims. "It's got to be my evil twin, Morgan. He always did say he was going to ruin Christmas by stealing from children instead of giving them gifts. He was always plotting and trying to come up with a spell. What was the word he kept using instead of Abracadabra?" He fought hard to think of the word in hopes that it would also be the magic word to reverse the spell. What *was* that word?

The sleigh was nearly unloaded, Santa's hands and feet were tied, and all the monster elves were gathering beside the sleigh. Santa, still trying to think of the magic word, was running out of time. He knew his brother must be arriving soon because the monster elves were coming to attention. "Riffraff. No, that's not it. Ripplemazoo. No, no, no. It started with an 'R' but I can't remember it."

Santa was getting more and more frustrated. As he was about to give up, he remembered and shouted it out, "Rizzlerazzlefrazzle!"

Suddenly, all the monster elves froze then dropped to the ground. "Cut!" yelled the director. "Scene five." While the stage hands were replacing the extras with the child actors already in makeup, the director continued.

"Thank you for your service, kids, you were great little monsters. Be sure to stop by the casting trailer to pick up your pay and verify your contact information."

"Wow!" Morach exclaimed excitedly. "That was an unbelievable experience. I've never been mean like that and have no desire to do it for real, but it was educational. I can see how someone seeing portions of movies could get the idea that happiness doesn't exist."

When Morach paused for a breath, Santa interjected, "I'm glad you had that experience, Morach. We should probably get you changed and collect your pay because your friends will be here soon. I'm afraid I'm going to have to leave you before they get here. I have some things to attend to at the workshop." Seeing the look on Morach's face turn downward, Santa quickly continued, "But I know we will meet again in a few weeks. Your friends need to observe more people in other  places before they see me.  Now go behind that trailer and quickly invoke your crystal before someone sees us."

"I'm sorry they didn't pick you to play Santa.  It was pretty ironic that they thought you didn't resemble the 'real' Santa, don't you think?"

"Yes, that was quite the surprise," Santa said chuckling.  True to the famous poem, his belly did shake like jelly.  "Ok, just tell the clerk inside to contact you through Santa's workshop at North Pole, Alaska. That's all the address they will need for now.  They will give you cash because you are from out-of-state.  I have to leave soon, so hurry in before everyone else gets here."

"I'll be back in a minute."  Morach came out a few minutes later and said his goodbyes to Santa.

"Now remember, I'll see you again on Christmas Eve," Santa said.  "There is much to do before then, so I need to go supervise and prepare.  Your friends will be here in a few minutes and will have lots of questions.

You'll know where to lead them when it's time."

"Thank you, Santa!" Morach said as he shook hands with Santa. "I appreciate all of your help. I think when I explain what you showed me to the others, they will see the error in the plan to destroy Earth. I'll see you soon!" Morach waved as Santa got in his RV and followed the other cars out of the studio lot.

Just then, he heard his name. "Morach!" Tony called while waving his arm. "There he is! Hey! Morach!" There were a few more snickers in the crowd when they thought Tony was calling a moron, but Morach and the other aliens ignored them.

Seeing the smiles on Tony's, Vedagy's, and Beeb's faces, Morach was indeed happy. "You were great!" Tony exclaimed when they met at the side of the crowd.

"We saw the whole scene you were in and most of the next one," Vedagy added.

"I can't believe they actually paid you to look like yourself," Beeb laughed. They glanced around quickly to make sure nobody heard that last comment. Nobody was paying attention to them because they were too involved with their own families. And that's what they had become, this committee of aliens – a family with all its problems, and bickering, and sharing, and working together.

"So this is where you ran off to without letting anyone know," Reyclebin admonished. "Did you not think any of us would become concerned or think someone had kidnapped you? I could have expected it from Beeb or Tony, but a renowned scientist such as you should know better."

With his head hung, Morach replied, "I apologize, Mr. President..." Reyclebin put out his hand and lifted Morach's chin as he reminded him to call him Rey, not Mr. President. "Yes, Sir, I mean, Rey."

"That's better. Now tell us what possessed you to come here and play an alien in a moving picture show."

"Can we hear this while we walk back to the park? We do have a mission to complete," Portamer complained.

"Of course, of course. Come along now. Limdon and Pumbint should have completed the repairs by now and we have more data to collect before we make a final recommendation."

"That's just it, Rey. I told you at the council meeting that I didn't feel the data was conclusive, right?" As everyone nodded their heads, Morach continued, "I came here because of a conversation I had with Mel – he's the salesman who sold me the maps of Hollywood. He told me:

A good movie is one that makes you feel something. Whether it's happiness, sadness, love, or hate, the intensity of those emotions determines how you relate to the story. It becomes a part of you and a really great movie lets you forget your own life for a little while as you become involved in the lives of the characters on the screen. People like to have adventure but don't always have the nerve, or the money, or even the time for it, so they escape into a movie to feel alive and free for a few hours.

You see, there has to be balance in the universe. There's the good and the bad in everything for everyone. Of course we all want the good and not the bad, but without the bad we wouldn't appreciate the good.   Some people need to be reminded of this and they get their emotions recharged during a great movie.

"So I had to visit the place they make movies to assess the validity of Mel's comments.  You saw the piece of movie that I was in.  It wasn't the full movie and it was the so-called bad part; but if you saw the whole thing all together, you would see that good ultimately wins.  We were only getting the middle parts of those movies, so all we saw was negativity and unhappiness."

"Yes, you have already said you didn't have full information when the council met.  I believe that is why we are here; to observe happiness first-hand so we are able to make an informed recommendation," Portamer said.

"You are correct, Portamer.  I am also impressed that Morach has found his voice.  I didn't know you had so much passion in you, Morach.  We will decide where to go next after we get some rest.  Ah, here we are.  How are the repairs coming along, Limmy?" Reyclebin asked.

"We just finished, Sir.  We should wait until tomorrow evening to do any        transformations, so the receptors have time to fully charge," Limdon answered.

"Sir, I've just heard from Frank," Frinkle announced excitedly. "He said Mr. Hardgold has a hotel right here in town and has made the penthouse suite available for our use tonight. It's just a few blocks away and has been fully stocked."

"Thanks, Frinkle," Reyclebin replied. "Let's get everything cleaned up so we can go to the hotel and relax for the evening. It has been a very eventful day,"

"I second that!" Limdon and Pumbint exclaimed in unison. They each had grease smudges on their noses and laughed when they noticed. Limdon reached over to wipe it off Pumbint's nose but it just smeared more.

"I'll wash it off when we get to the hotel," Pumbint said with a smile and a twinkle in his eyes. Everyone got to work clearing the area and stowing the spare parts so people wouldn't even know they had been there.

Name:  Beeb (beeb)
Nickname:  Beeb
Planet:  Sniggins (snig-ins)
Galaxy:  Snipkpins (snip-ins)
Specialty:  Writer
Dietary Needs:  no restrictions
  » Chocolate acts like alcohol
Other:
  » Won the lottery to become a member of the committee
  » All names in his galaxy are spelled the same frontwards and backwards
  » Record keeper for this mission

# Beeb's Fourth Report

Galactic Day 4 –

*This has been a long day. We are still in the United States of America. At T minus 672 we left San Francisco, California, in search of replacement parts to repair the ship. We began traveling along the highways toward Hollywood, California, and continued to look for parts in each town we passed through – but were unable to locate any.*

*The fog and steep streets in San Francisco were making ~~Reyclebin~~ Mr. President ill, but he recovered as soon as we left the area with all the hills (or did he recover because of the anti-nausea herbs Vedagy had given him?) Everyone was wishing we could fly again.*

*We finally arrived in Hollywood and stopped at a mall for information. Some of the committee was able to directly interact with the locals: Portamer learned that people show their happiness in different ways, Morach learned the significance of movies and how they impact the lives of humans.*

*Morach also obtained a map of Hollywood and found a park near the hardware store. Fortunately, the hardware store had all of the parts Limdon and Pumbint needed to repair the ship. While they were working on the repairs, Morach wandered off to a place called Universal Studios to find out more about how movies are transmitted. .*

*They are sent by signal to a big satellite outside Earth's atmosphere where they are retransmitted to other satellites and back to Earth for other areas to enjoy. It was these transmissions that we intercepted. Apparently, the data collectors were reviewing only the bad parts of movies, which led them to conclude there was no happiness here. While that is still to be determined, it shows the data was indeed incomplete*

*When it was discovered that Morach was not in camp, all but Clombic, Limdon, and Pumbint went to the Universal Studio to look for him. It turns out he was paid to appear in a movie! He played the part of an Alien in a plot to capture Santa Claus. It was scary, but we saw that Santa was saved and everyone was happy at the end of the movie. When we returned to the ship, the repairs had been completed.*

*Frinkle received a message from his cousin Frankle in New York who said his employer, Mr.*

Hardgold, had a hotel in Hollywood and we were invited to stay for a couple of nights if we wanted. Everyone was happy to hear this because all of us were tired. We are not quite half-way through our mission but it has been interesting. We haven't even left the United States of America, yet. We will be meeting tomorrow to plan our next destination.

This concludes my report for galactic day four on the S.H.A.D.E. mission.

# *Profile – Pumbint*

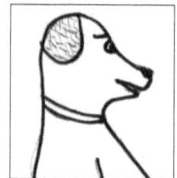

Name:  Pumbint (pum-bint)
Nickname:  Punt
Planet:  Edabel (eed-uh-bell)
Galaxy:  Nougat (new-gut)
Specialty:  Master of Electronics
Dietary Needs:

» Meat & vegetables – no sugar

Other:

» Invented the communication portion of the coms unit
» Altered the ship to enable transforming into alternate modes of transportation
» Can repair any electronic device

ten

# Limdon and Pumbint's Secret

Everyone had been waiting for Pumbint and Limdon. They tried contacting the two on their coms units to no avail. Were they in trouble? The committee was meeting at the ship in 10 minutes and everyone else was assembled.

"I'm going back to the suite. Maybe they forgot something."

"Good idea, Frinkle, I'll come with you," Clombic said as they headed back to the suite. "Rey is going to be angry if they don't show up at the ship on time."

"Here we are. You check that side, I'll check this one..." she heard something coming from the bathroom. "Frinkle, over here. I heard something." Frinkle joined Clombic just as she knocked on the bedroom door. "Hello? Who's in there?" They heard a sharp intake of breath and hurried whispering, but couldn't make out the voices. Clombic opened the door with her taser in her hand, ready to attack.

"Whoa, Cloe, it's me, Limmy..."

"and Pumbint," he finished.

"Wow!" Frinkle exclaimed. "I never would have expected that! What are you doing in there?"

They were on their hands and knees in the middle of the bathroom floor. "We were just trying to put my crystal back together. I dropped it and the main crystal dislodged. I can't go out looking like this, can I?" Limdon didn't look human without the crystal. She was in her natural form as a planet Conog citizen. Long, pink hair covered her body. She had green arms and legs and a green face with pink eyebrows and blue eyes. Her green ears were like a cat's and stood on top of her head. Her pink jumpsuit complemented her coloring nicely.

"Nooooo, I don't think you could blend like that, but Frinkle has a crystal and he can blend in his natural form," Clombic supplied.

"Yeah, here, Lim, Frank doesn't use a crystal and he passes as human. You can at least get back to the ship for the meeting and you can repair it there."

"Right! The meeting! Oh, we have to hurry. Pumbint, darling, did you get everything?"

"Darling?" Frinkle and Clombic said in unison with surprised looks on their faces.

"Now you've done it," Pumbint grimaced. "We'll be in front of the inter-galactic firing squad within minutes of landing."

"What's going on? Are you two dating?" Frinkle asked in awe.

"You would have found out sooner or later anyway. Lim never could keep a secret for very long. We are married. Now that you know, let's get to the ship. The meeting is about to start and we can't be late. Could you keep this to yourselves until we tell Mr. President?"

"Ok, I'll try my best. I am really bad about keeping secrets, so you should probably tell him right after the meeting," Frinkle said sadly. They returned to the ship together – just in time for the meeting to start.

"Good morning."

"Good morning, Sir," came the replies amidst various yawns.

"I trust you slept well and had a fortifying breakfast? Thank you, Veda, for your continued culinary services."

"You're welcome, Sir; but I have to give credit to my helpers Tony, Beeb, and Frinkle, as well," Vedagy replied. She smiled when she saw the pink cheeks of her helpers. They were remembering the mishap during the preparations that morning. Frinkle and Tony were trying to get Vedagy to let them flip the pancakes – until she finally gave in and let each of them flip one. Frinkle flipped his hard and it landed on the griddle...mostly. The uncooked side splattered all over him – causing a round of laughter. Tony was still laughing when it was his turn, so he wasn't paying attention. He flipped the pancake high in the air and it fell right on top of his head! Of course, this caused more laughter and more mess to clean up.

Beeb, seeing the fun, had to have a turn as well. He didn't want to flip it too hard and get splattered and he didn't want to flip it too high and have it fall on him; so he did it very slowly and close to the griddle. While it stayed on the griddle and didn't splat, it didn't exactly turn over completely, either. It just folded in half. Of course, he was embarrassed when the other boys laughed; but he felt better when Vedagy said it was the best of all of them because she could unfold it and it was still edible. The other two were tossed in the sink to cool before being put in the garbage.

"You are very generous, Veda," Reyclebin grinned. Vedagy smiled and winked at the three helpers.

"Now," he continued, "the ship is repaired and we thank Limmy and Punt for their expertise in this matter." Smiles and nods of acknowledgement were exchanged. "We have been here over three galactic days now and are still in North America. We need to see other continents to obtain additional data. Our original itinerary has been discarded due to our recent delays. However, we need to visit South America and then move to the Eastern hemisphere for further study. Does anyone have any preferences or suggestions?" he asked. Not seeing any immediate responses, he said, "Ok, I will point to a place on the map and that's where we will go next. Captain, could you bring the Earth map, please?"

The captain brought the map and laid it out on the table. It hung over the sides, so Reyclebin folded it with South America facing up. He closed his eyes, moved his hand in a figure eight as if to mix it up, and pointed to… Uruguay. *Uruguay?* Tony thought. *Where the heck is Uruguay?*

"Well, it appears Uruguay is our next destination. Portamer, could you get some information on this country for us? It appears to be rather small. Find out which city is the largest so we have a more refined destination. Thank you."

"Certainly, Sir, I will start immediately." Portamer turned his chair to face the console and began his research on Uruguay.

The console was made up of several screens with keyboards and knobs. Each screen had its own purpose. The one farthest left was dedicated to the coms systems. It monitored each member's life support system, provided the links to their individual coms units, and showed how much charge was left on each unit. Every time a member was onboard, they removed their units and set them on specialized pads to recharge with energy collected from the moon. (Although the moon's energy was strong enough to charge the coms units, it couldn't recharge the ship's power crystals.) The coms units were currently charging – except Limdon's, which was still broken.

The screen to the right of the coms station was linked to Earth's satellites so they could monitor the weather and navigate the safest routes. The captain also consulted this monitor before transforming – to minimize any damages. He didn't consult it last time, which is why a receptacle was damaged.

The center screen controlled everything else. It was the one they used to transform the ship into a bus, plane, helicopter, boat, and back to their space ship. They could transform anywhere. It monitored the receptacles and showed how much power was available and whether or not they were currently charging. It also controlled the louvers that opened to the sun's strongest rays. The louvers then closed at night and during bad weather to protect the receptacles. It was all rather complicated and required training to operate. The captain, Reyclebin, Limdon, and Pumbint were the   only ones qualified to operate the center screen.

The next screen was a dedicated surveillance system. It showed images from cameras (located around the perimeter of the ship) to watch for intruders. After-all, they were in their true forms aboard ship and didn't want to be seen this way by humans – except by Tony, of course. It also allowed them to remain undetected by radar when flying and sonar when sailing. They had to protect themselves against unknown situations.

The last screen was farthest right. This was where Portamer was accessing the satellites and the world wide web of information. This screen was always connected and available to any member onboard. Portamer was searching and listening to the meeting at the same time.

*Frank. Frank, are you there?* Frinkle was attempting to contact his cousin to get his input.

*I'm here, Frinkle. How was your stay last night?*

*It was great! We had fun at breakfast and then found out Limdon and Pumbint are married. Oh, I'm not supposed to say anything yet, but at least nobody else can hear me.* Frinkle smiled at that thought.

*Really?! I thought there was something going*

*on between those two. I saw how they looked at each other.*

*Yeah, it was a total surprise to me. But that's not why I'm calling. We are deciding where to go next and Mr. President, Rey, randomly chose Uruguay. Do you know anything about that country?*

*Not much. What I do know is that it's the second smallest country in South America – down by Argentina – and Santa Claus is called Papa Noel. It's summertime there now. Oh, and it doesn't snow there... ever.*

*Ok, thanks, Frank. I have to go now. I'll talk to you soon and let you know how things are going.*

*Nice hearing from you, Frinkle. Say hello to everyone. Bye.*

"Portamer, do you have anything yet?" Reyclebin asked.

"Not enough yet, Sir. May I have a few more minutes?"

"Certainly."

"Uh, Sir? I just spoke with Frank and he told me the little bit he knows about Uruguay," Frinkle said.

"Go ahead. What have you learned?" Reyclebin encouraged.

"Well, Sir, everyone, the only things he

could tell me is that it's a very small country and it never snows there. That's good news, right? Then you can join us outside," he said with a smile.

"That is what I found, too, Sir," Portamer added. "The capital is Montevideo and I would suggest we go there. Approximately half of the population of the entire country lives there. I also read that they are preparing for Christmas even though it doesn't snow. They seem to use fireworks to distract the children while Santa Claus...excuse me...Papa Noel, as he is called there, delivers happiness at midnight on Christmas Eve."

"Oh, right! Frank mentioned that, too." Frinkle interrupted and received a frown from Portamer.

"As we are on a mission to find happiness, I agree that we should go to Montevideo," Reyclebin said. "Portamer, you and the captain should work on the proper transportation mode and route. Veda, could you take your helpers to the market to replenish supplies?" Seeing her nod of agreement, he continued, "Cloe, you can look for any obstacles we may encounter so we are prepared. Limdon and Pumbint and I have other things to discuss.

Everyone is to meet back here before dark. Meeting adjourned."

Everyone leaving the ship turned on their coms units and proceeded to fulfill their assigned tasks. Limdon had reattached her crystal and was now testing the components. It seemed to be working properly. She, Pumbint, and Reyclebin went outside to walk to a nearby park. Reyclebin knew something was on their minds because they had been exceptionally quiet during the meeting.

"Ok, you two, let me hear it."

"Um, how did you know, Sir?" Pumbint asked.

"I don't know. What I *do* know is that something is bothering the two of you because it isn't like you to be this quiet during a meeting. Is there a problem with the receptacles that I should be aware of?"

"Oh, no, Sir!" they said in unison. Limdon continued, "The ship is perfectly fine, Sir. This is of a personal nature and we don't know how to say it."

"The best way is to just say it, Lim," Pumbint said. "Sir, we have a secret." Pumbint took hold of Limdon's hand and looked into her eyes lovingly as he said, "We are married." They both looked at their leader with fear of the consequences of keeping this a secret.

"Is that all?" Reyclebin laughed. "I thought it was something bad." He cleared his throat then said sternly, "You do know that if I had known this before we left the council that I wouldn't have been able to bring the both of you along?"

"Yes, Sir," Limdon said. "That's why we couldn't tell you before. We work great together and this mission needed both of us."

"I agree, but the rules clearly stated that only one citizen per galaxy was allowed..." he began.

"Yes, Sir, we understand that," Pumbint interrupted. "But, you see, we *are* citizens of different galaxies. We spend half of the year in her galaxy and half in mine. That way, we maintain our respective citizenship for our families' sake and we can contribute to each of our galaxies, who depend on our expertise."

"Well, since you are citizens of different galaxies, I don't see that there is a problem. It is almost cheating, but is legal. You can feel assured you won't have any repercussions when we return to the council."

"Thank you, Sir." They sighed in relief as they shook Reyclebin's hands and beamed with joy.

"Now, stop trying so hard to hide it and let's make sure we have everything we need for the next phase of our mission." Reyclebin gave them each a hug and they walked back to the ship to check that the ship's mechanics were in proper working order and to make sure they had ample replacement parts should they be needed. After all, the parts may or may not be readily available in other countries.

# *Profile – Vedagy*

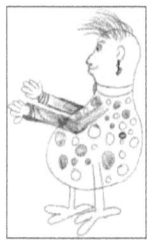

Name: Vedagy (ved-uh-gee)
Nickname: Veda
Planet: Noslew (no-sloo)
Galaxy: Rutaby (root-uh-bee)
Specialty: Master of Herbs
Dietary Needs: Vegetarian
Other:

» Can identify any plant to determine if it is poisonous, edible, or has healing qualities
» Knows how to cook and heal using any vegetable or herb

## eleven

# *Uruguay*

It was a good thing they hadn't checked out of the hotel yet because they needed to stay another night while they completed their preparations. All food was stored, spare parts were secured, and maps were made. They were finally ready to leave the USA.

"What do ya mean there may be a problem, Portamer?" Clombic asked.

"Relax, Clombic, there hasn't been any political unrest in that country for over a century," he replied. "We simply do not have any passports or documentation. However, we may be able to get around this if we land in the rural area and drive to the city. Most of the country's commerce is agricultural – supplemented with tourism and services such as technical support relocated from other countries. The services and tourism are largely centered around the main cities (the largest of which is Montevideo on the south-ern coast – our destination) leaving the majority of this small country as farmland. If we land in a field of cows or sheep away from population, we should not have any prob-lems."

"Remember, Portamer, our coms units disguise us to look like the locals and our speech is heard in whatever language the listener understands," Limdon commented.

"Also," Pumbint added, "when the ship transforms it is disguised as one of the local means of transportation so we blend in."

"Of course, this is why I suggested landing in a field rather than arriving by private yacht or airplane. We can then avoid questions regarding our nationality and origins," Portamer said. "We can calculate approximate coordinates until we get closer, then we can locate the appropriate landing field when we have a better view of the actual landscape."

"Very well done, everyone," Reyclebin praised. "Good job, Portamer. Thank you for your thorough research as always. Ok, Captain, let's be on our way."

"Yes, Sir. It will take several hours to get

there, so I suggest everyone sit back and relax."

After a couple of hours, Vedagy and her helpers prepared a light meal. Although light meal was a bit of an understatement with the variety of foods she had to serve, everyone had the perfect amount and was neither hungry nor over filled. Some did take naps afterwards as was their custom on their home planets.

Shortly after sunrise, Uruguay appeared on the radar. Portamer and Reyclebin checked the monitor and scanned the countryside for a possible landing area. "Here's one," Reyclebin said as he pointed to the screen. "There doesn't appear to be much livestock in that particular field and it's close to the city."

"Unfortunately, it appears there are crops planted there..." Portamer was interrupted by Tony's burst of laughter. "What is so funny, Tony?"

"If we landed in the middle of a field of corn, we would make crop circles," he said between fits of laughter. Seeing the perplexed look on everyone's faces, he explained in a somewhat sobered manner, "There was a science fiction movie years ago, that showed circles that mysteriously appeared in the middle of wheat fields. Everyone was saying the circles were caused by an alien ship landing in the middle of the fields." Tony started laughing again as understanding dawned on Portamer's face, followed by impatience. "See, it would be true if we landed there 'cause you're aliens." By now, some of the others were giggling as well.

"Be that as it may, Tony, we will not be landing in the middle of a field making... crop circles. That is the last kind of attention we want to draw from the authorities." Turning back to the monitor, Portamer found a suitable landing site and relayed the coordinates to the captain as everyone fastened their safety belts and made sure their coms units were firmly in place. Within minutes, they had landed and the ship was transformed into a bus that looked like it had seen better days.

The first thing everyone noticed was the heat. It was approximately 78 degrees, according to Portamer, but the humidity made it feel much hotter. There was a very light breeze which gave little relief. Fortunately, their suits adjusted their body temperatures quickly, so they were comfortable within minutes – including Tony, who was wearing his new suit and grinning proudly when it cooled him down.

Clombic quickly claimed the front seat to scout for signs of trouble. Tony asked her why she was holding a water gun. The weapon she was holding looked like one he had seen at Sterling's Toy Store in Manhattan last year. Of course, Clombic couldn't be bothered to say more than, "It is *not* a water gun and definitely *not* a toy." Reyclebin, upon hearing the exchange, told Clombic to put the weapon away.

"But, Sir," Clombic protested. "I know Portamer said there wasn't any political unrest, but who's to say there aren't local bandits?"

"I know you are doing your job to protect us, Cloe, but we don't want to give the locals the wrong impression. Remember, we are here to find signs of happiness – not to provoke the locals to become hostile because you are brandishing a firearm. Now, put it away."

"Yes, Sir," she said as she reluctantly stowed the gun. She reclaimed her seat and continued watching for signs of trouble while they traveled the dusty, bumpy, dirt road on their way to the city.

Vedagy, Beeb, Tony, and Frinkle were pointing out things they saw along the road. "Over there!" Tony shouted excitedly, "It's a hummingbird!" True enough, a hummingbird dressed in green and red hovered over a bright yellow flower. It flew out of perceived danger until the bus passed. "Did you see it?" Beeb and Frinkle saw it, but Vedagy didn't. They continued to point out animals in the bushes and trees that provided a semi barrier between the road and the fields and pastures beyond. They saw armadillos, deer, cows, sheep, and even an old owl sleeping in a tree.

As they approached the outskirts of Montevideo, the sun was starting to set and lights were coming on. Some of the private homes already had colored lights hung for the upcoming Christmas celebrations.

A young boy darted onto the road in front of the bus; and the captain stopped just in time to miss hitting the boy and his mother – who had run after the boy. The mother wore a pale cotton skirt, sandals, brightly colored blouse, and a matching bandana on her head. She held her son closely to her chest while thanking the captain and muttering a prayer of thanks that her child was unharmed. Oblivious as to why his mother was crying, the young boy lay in his mother's arms and sucked on the large necklace of beads she wore. People were outside within seconds, offering refreshments to the strangers who hadn't run over the boy. They were just putting breakfast on the table for their entire family (including aunts, uncles, cousins, and grandparents – twenty-six in all).

Amazed at the amount of attention and happiness displayed, the committee was honored to accompany the boy's family into their home. Clombic surveyed the premises for weapons and, finding nothing threatening, relaxed to enjoy the scene. Two elderly men with leathered, tan faces were playing a card game.

"Antonio, put the cards away and come greet our guests!" one of the ladies scolded.

"Hello, guests, thank you for saving my nephew. Enjoy some food," Antonio yelled back with no intention of rising from the card game. "Maria, we are at game point and I have only one card left. I'll be there soon." Portamer was intrigued by the intense focus of this Antonio person, so he had to observe the game.

"Hello, young man," Horatio greeted. Horatio was the other player and was holding three cards close to his chest. Laid on the table in front of each of them were rows of cards in different denominations. Some were stacked and others were fanned out. In the middle of the table were two piles – one face-up and one face-down. The face-down pile had only a few cards left in it. Antonio took two cards from the face-down pile and looked at them. He laid one down on the row with the corresponding number then stacked the cards into a pile.

"Canasta! No wilds!" Antonio said excitedly. He had three other similar piles so why this should be a cause for celebration was unknown to Portamer, who continued to watch. Antonio laid one of his remaining two cards on the face-up pile, which Horatio quickly picked up. There were five cards in the pile he picked up. He added them to his other cards after laying the top card, along with two from his hand, on the table in front of him. With a grin, he laid down another three cards in a group; laid a joker on top of another row; and laid down his final card in the center of the table – next to the two remaining face-down cards.

"And I'm out! Ha!" Horatio whooped and, seeing the look on Antonio's face, laughed harder. They tallied the points for the cards lying in front of each of them and, although Antonio won the hand, Horatio won the game by 210 points. With grumblings from Antonio, Horatio got up from the table and put his arm around Portamer's shoulders, which startled him. As they walked toward the dining room, Horatio apologized for ignoring the guests.

Maria gave Portamer a plate and pushed one into Horatio's hand while commenting to the others, "You would think these two invented the game the way they carry on so. Just because it was invented in Montevideo in the mid nineteenth century, they act like it makes the world go around." She smiled as she said this, though. It seemed to be an ongoing family joke.

"Now, now, Maria. We were raised on Canasta. We owe it to our ancestors, who invented this game, to pass it down to the next generation; which means we have to stay in practice – so we can beat them!" Antonio chimed in as he took a plate and joined the buffet line.

Vedagy had been talking to Theresa about the foods being served, while watching the reactions of her fellow committee members for which dishes they enjoyed most. Tony seemed to enjoy all of it – apparently there isn't anything Tony *doesn't* like. Limdon and Pumbint chose the tortas (essentially, grilled ham and cheese sandwiches) and asado (basically a type of barbecued beef with a special chimichurri sauce made of water, oil, and a variety of savory herbs). Clombic liked the asado and croissants and also chose a dulce de leche filled crepe (sweet, thickened milk also known as milk caramel). Portamer, needing his sugar, chose a few dulce de leche filled crepes drowned with maple syrup and seemed to be enjoying them immensely. *Note to self: learn how to make dulce de leche crepes for Portamer's birthday.*

Vedagy continued watching everyone's choices as she enjoyed her own food. She chose brioche (a type of buttery bread roll) stuffed with cheese and grilled red peppers; eggs scrambled with red peppers, onions, and mushrooms; and dulce de leche crepes. She and Reyclebin chose yerba mate for their beverage. They were told it was a magical drink made from the yerba mate plant: ground up, put in a cup, water added, and drunk through a bamboo straw – kind of like a tea. They had to stop Tony, Frinkle, and Beeb from trying the espresso, because the three already had enough energy to power the ship – if they could siphon it, that is. They were given orange juice instead.

After enjoying the hospitality of this family and seeing how happy they were just to be among family and share their home and food with strangers, the committee said goodbye and proceeded to Montevideo. They found many homes with people hanging strings of colored lights and putting up Christmas decorations. Children were laughing and playing in the streets in bare feet. The bared feet was a shock to Portamer because he could clearly see the discarded shoes piled on the side of the road. *I will never understand Earth customs*, he thought. *Why these children would not wear perfectly good shoes to protect their feet is beyond me.* What Portamer didn't know is that these particular children were having a contest as to who could stay on the street without shoes the longest. Three of the five children were        already putting their shoes back on.  The last two were hopping around, but refused to be the first to reclaim his shoes – making him the loser.

Hearing the chatter as they turned the corner, they found dozens of people walking down the street while vendors were calling to them to buy their items.  Of course, the committee had to get a better look to experience this phenomenon.  There were so many people in the street it was hard to keep together, so they agreed to meet at the bus in one hour and report on their findings.  Limdon gave each member – including Tony – $20.00 to spend.  "Now spend it wisely and remember that we have limited room for traveling," Limdon reminded them.  She and Pumbint smiled at each other; thinking of the children they would have one day.

"One more thing," Portamer said, catching them before they disbursed.  "Our mission is to determine happiness, so do not forget why we are here."

"Spoilsport," Tony muttered under his breath before he smiled and grabbed the hands of his best friends, Beeb and Frinkle.  They wandered around and looked at every table they saw. One had T-shirts with funny sayings on them, such as: "Uruguay – Home of Canasta!" Antonio would like that one; "I'm a girl and Uruguay – let's party!" for the vacationers; "I'm going Uruguay...Want a ride?" for the surfing enthusiasts. Another booth had freshly harvested fruits and vegetables, while yet another had seashells with faces painted on them. Some of the seashells were even attached to hair combs. The boys decided they would get one for Vedagy for all the kindness she showed them.

Vedagy was drawn to the booth selling dresses. They were made of cotton, which was cooling in the humid days. She was very interested in the colors. Knowing the dresses were made for Earthling body shapes and hers was nothing like them, she still purchased a particularly large dress that she could alter to fit her own body.

Limdon and Pumbint meandered through the crowd together and stopped at a table selling charms and crystals. Limdon, knowing a lot about crystals, was intrigued by the small size of them. Her planet had crystals, but the smallest was the size of a golf ball. These were the size of peas. Apparently, they had been pre-cut. The ones in their coms units had been cut to the size and shape needed. However, she was still drawn to the pink quartz because it was not very plentiful on her planet – even though it was the most universal in its qualities. She decided to buy a few of the larger pieces (the size of a small baseball). Pumbint spotted a table selling tools and had to have a complete screw driver and wrench set. He could never have enough tools in his line of work.

The others wound their way through the street but didn't find anything to purchase. They did, however, witness a few acts of kindness... in particular, a vendor gave a little girl a charm bracelet for just one peso when the price was marked at five pesos. She was buying it for a Christmas present for her sick mother.

It was almost time to meet at the bus, so each group began making their way back. Suddenly, someone shouted, "Stop! Thief!" Clombic turned toward the voice and saw the vendor pointing at her. The vendor had seen her coms unit and thought it was stolen. He tried to take it from her so she used her self-defense   karate chop after trying to tell him it was hers and she didn't steal it. He, in fact, was a thief trying to steal it from her. In the struggle, it was loosened enough that her image was flashing between her true form and her projected Earth form.

Limdon, Pumbint, and Reyclebin were nearby and witnessed the whole thing. They immediately came to Clombic's assistance and held the man while Limdon secured the coms unit. Clombic's projection was stable once again. Bystanders noticed they were all wearing the same necklace and told the vendor he needed proof that the necklace was stolen. Knowing he had no proof, he hung his head and went back to his booth to pack up for the day. He doubted he would get any more sales from this crowd after that display.

Limdon activated her coms link and sent a message to all the others. *Meet at the bus immediately. We have a situation and need to vacate the area. We are not in danger. Repeat. We are not in danger but we will be leaving in five minutes.*

The captain was also connected to the coms link. Upon hearing the announcement, he started warming up the bus and took it to the rendezvous site. He had parked several blocks away because of the bazaar, but was now back at the drop off point – awaiting their return.  As soon as everyone was onboard and accounted for, the captain drove back toward the empty field they had landed in to carry-out the procedures set in place for such a situation – make sure everyone is safe then leave the area to avoid conflict with the locals.

The captain and Pumbint did the pre-flight preparations and took off as quickly as possible while everyone stowed their purchases and got settled in.  They went into invisible mode until they were far over the Atlantic Ocean – at which time, they turned off the invisible mode to conserve their energy.  With the solar panels fixed, they weren't in danger of running out of power, but it was always a good idea to be cautious.

"Where are we going now," Tony asked after they had been in flight for an hour. Everyone had been quietly reflecting on the events at the bazaar.  Now it was time to plan for the next adventure.

"We are going east," Pumbint said.

"Let's look at the map to see what's East," Tony said to Beeb.  They went to the console where Portamer had the world map on the screen.  If they continued due East, they would just miss the southern-most tip of Africa.

"When we get closer to Africa, we will turn north and visit a country there," Reyclebin added.

"Cool. Can we go to Egypt? They have the pyramids there," Tony commented.

"It will be several hours until we get that far, but we will keep it in mind," Rey said.

Name:  Pader (pay-der)
Nickname:  Captain
Planet:  Geeter (ghee-ter)
Galaxy:  Buffinger (buff-een-jer)
Specialty:  Intergalactic Travel
Dietary Needs:  no restrictions
Other:

> » Has flown a shuttle between galaxies for many years
> » Friends with Reyclebin and his wife
> » Studied driving laws for all  galaxies

twelve

# *Africa*

As the sun was rising, Tony awoke and looked out the window. He rubbed the sleep out of his eyes and looked again. There was sand as far as he could see. He went to another window and saw more of the same. Acres and acres of rolling, golden sand filled the view from every vantage point.

He found Pumbint and Portamer at the command console with the captain. "Where are we, Portamer?" Tony asked.

"Not now, Tony," Portamer began. "We seem to be having some difficulty with the computers and communications."

Reyclebin walked over just in time to hear Portamer's comment. Laying a hand on Tony's shoulder, he said, "It's okay, Tony. Why don't you go see if you can help Veda with breakfast? We'll have a meeting when we have more information."

"Okay, I'll wait for the meeting," he agreed with a disappointed tone. He went off to see what he could pilfer from Vedagy while she was making breakfast.

"Now, what is this I hear about difficulty?"

"Our communications and positioning systems are not responding, Sir. Pumbint thinks it may have a sickness…"

"It's called a virus, Portamer. I'm surprised you didn't know that, being a    Professor."

"Yes, well, I don't teach computer systems, Pumbint. So what does it mean for our systems to have a virus?"

"Simply put, it is sick," he said with a smirk, but seeing the look on Portamer's face, he hurried on. "I am reversing the damage to the time before the virus took effect. It will take a bit for it to run. Then I will have to do additional diagnostics to make sure it is updated to our current status."

"Captain, do you know where we are? We seem to be surrounded by a lot of sand," Reyclebin asked.

"Uh… I'm sorry, Sir. I think I dozed off

for an hour. When I awoke, the navigation system was not responding, so I landed here. Fortunately, the navigation and communications systems do not affect the power or manual flying controls."

"I see. I suppose it is a good thing we didn't end up in the ocean then. Keep me informed of the progress, Pumbint. I will send Limdon in with breakfast for you when it is ready. Is there anything else you need?"

"Thank you, Sir. I don't believe I need anything else at the moment. Limdon may be able to help with the crystals for the communications system, though."

With a nod, Reyclebin started to leave the command center but paused to ask the captain to join him in the conference room. The captain, unable to meet Reyclebin's eyes, took a seat opposite him.

"Pader," Reyclebin began calmly, "I am not upset that you fell asleep. What I would like to know is what happened up until that time and what you can remember about where we were headed before the navigation system failed."

With obvious relief, Pader looked at Reyclebin and told him that the last thing he remembered was they were heading for Africa. "I think that's where we are, but *where* in Africa is unknown. It appears we are in one of their deserts, but I have no idea in which direction we should go from here. Pumbint says we shouldn't travel until the systems are repaired."

"Do you remember seeing anything beyond the sand before you landed?"

"Well, I believe there is a village and some sort of water, possibly a river or lake, to the East but I am not sure how far it is from here."

"I think I will have a few of the committee members go up to the top of the sand hill for a better view. If the village isn't far, we may 'check it out' as Tony would say. Thank you, Pader. You may get some breakfast and, if Pumbint doesn't need your immediate help, get some rest."

"Thank you, Sir. I'm sorry I fell asleep." With a weary look and a slump to his shoulders, Pader left Reyclebin with his thoughts.

\* \* \* \* \*

Everyone met in the conference room after breakfast. "It appears we had some technical difficulties just before we landed," Reyclebin began. "Pumbint, how are the repairs progressing?"

"Communication is restored, thanks to Limmy's help..."

"It was just a couple of jarred crystals. They don't get viruses like computers and people do." Limdon interrupted. Her cheeks grew pink as she realized she had interrupted his report. With an apologetic smile, she let Pumbint continue.

"And the navigational system will be repaired in a few hours... um... that is... two or three Earth days." Everyone began talking at once and looking at each other with concern and panic.

"What?"

"There's nothing but sand, what are we going to do for three days?"

"Where are we?"

"Do we have enough supplies?"

Holding his hands up to get their attention, Reyclebin took control of the meeting again. "Quiet down. Quiet down. There's no reason to panic."

As the voices faded, Tony asked, "Are we in Egypt? I see a lot of sand, but I don't see the pyramids."

"We believe we are on the continent of Africa but are unable to pinpoint our exact location at this time. I don't think we are near Egypt, but we do believe there is a village a short distance from here – which brings me to our next item on the agenda.

"I would like a small party to go to the top of the sand hill to the East and determine if the village is within walking range. Clombic, Veda, Beeb, and Tony will be going – unless there are any objections?" Reyclebin asked as he looked at each of the four in turn.

Clombic was already planning what weapons to take and Vedagy was wondering what herbs she would find in the village. Beeb was smiling shyly, while trying not to show the excitement and fear he was feeling at one time. Tony, of course, was smiling widely and could hardly wait to be dismissed, so they could get going. This irritated Portamer. *Why did we have to bring him along? He is disrupting this meeting again.*

"I would like to go, too, if I may," Morach requested. "I'd like to see if Santa has been here yet."

"You may go as well, Mark, but I have no information regarding Santa in this part of

Earth's population. Remember, you are to report to me when you have reached the top of the hill, so we can determine if the travel is feasible."

"Yes, Sir," they all replied at once.

"Unless there is anything else..." Reyclebin looked around the room for signs of questions. Seeing none, he continued. "...you should be ready to leave within the hour. Limdon will be monitoring the communications and keeping me apprised."

Reyclebin, Pumbint, Limdon and Portamer went back to the control center while the others prepared for their departure.

\* \* \* \* \*

"Stay here while I take a look over the crest of the hill. We don't know what we will find," Clombic said as she prepared her bow and pulled an arrow in case she needed to use it. She made her way to the top of the hill and crawled the last few feet. Raising her head, she saw the village Reyclebin had mentioned. It was less than a mile away and easily travelled in under an hour. She didn't see any signs of militia on the perimeter, so she made her way back to the others and contacted the ship.

*Limmy, this is Cloe. Are you there?*

*Yes, I'm here. Rey is here with me and you are on the overhead. We can see that you are at the top of the hill. What did you find?*

*The village is less than a mile away and easily travelled in under an hour. I didn't see any militia on the perimeter and it doesn't appear hostile. What are your orders, Sir?*

*If you feel it is safe, go ahead and explore the village; but keep us informed. Please try to be back before it gets dark.*

*We will be, Sir. We will contact you again when we get to the village.* With that done, Clombic relayed the conversation to the rest of the group. She had to stop Tony from running ahead as he continually wanted to do. Vedagy laughed at his exuberance.

"Tony, why don't you run back here and help me up the hill. My stride is not as long as yours." It wasn't that Vedagy had any problems keeping up with the others, but she felt it would distract Tony from annoying Clombic, who was on alert. Beeb started laughing as Tony tripped and fell in the sand.

Tony got up and brushed himself off, then started running toward Beeb. Knowing what

Tony had in mind, Beeb started running away from him. They chased each other until they were almost to the village. Clombic and Vedagy were glad the boys had worn themselves out so they weren't as flighty while they were in the village.

They walked into the main square about noon and saw several vendors. Limdon had given them some money to buy supplies with and (after letting Reyclebin know they had arrived at the village unharmed) they used a little to get some lunch.

At the end of the street, they chose a small hut with two guest tables outside. One table was already occupied, so they quickly sat down at the other. They observed the people at the other table to learn their customs for ordering. Fortunately, they had remembered to make a translator for Tony so he could also understand the native language.

Veda ordered a vegetarian dish of white corn and beans. Clombic chose the beef and lamb meatloaf with yellow rice and a rich sauce. Tony, Morach and Beeb decided on a simple beef stew. Their lunches were served with a mild beer for the ladies and Morach, and fresh cow's milk for the boys. They finished their meal and thanked their hosts before making their way through the villagers to visit the rest of the market stalls.

Vedagy found some herbs she hadn't been able to get in the United States, and some she was running low on, so she had to stock up. Clombic kept her eye out for any signs of trouble while the boys helped Vedagy by carrying the packages of purchased supplies. Before long, Clombic told them they needed to return to the ship.

They filled their water jugs and arranged their purchases on something resembling a stretcher used to carry injured soldiers during the war. It was a piece of sturdy cloth approximately three feet wide by four feet long strung between two poles and carried by two people. As Clombic was the one protecting them, she needed to have her hands free and did not take a turn at carrying the supplies. The boys were growing more and more tired as they neared the ship. Just before they topped the ridge leading to the ship, Tony let out a scream and dropped his end of the stretcher.

Beeb and Vedagy ran to Tony while Clombic went on full alert looking for the source of the attack. Tony was crying and holding his ankle, saying he had been bitten. Vedagy looked at the affected area and determined it was a sting, not a bite. She quickly looked around and saw a scorpion a few feet away. It appeared to be returning to its colony. Vedagy pulled Clombic aside and told her she needed to treat Tony's leg quickly, but they had to move away from the scorpion colony or they could all be stung. Tony would be losing feeling in his leg soon if she didn't get it treated. Clombic said she would carry him if Morach and Beeb could manage the supplies.

They made it to the top of the hill and saw the ship below them. Vedagy agreed they were safely away from the scorpion's colony and she asked Clombic to set Tony on the stretcher. She and Beeb moved some of the supplies out of the way to make room for Tony. Clombic immediately activated her coms unit to a telepathic channel for Reyclebin's ears only. After relaying the situation, she saw Portamer and Pumbint on their way up the hill with an extra stretcher and bandages.

By the time they reached the top, Vedagy

had cleansed the site and began making a poultice of herbs she had purchased at the village market. She was happy she had decided to stock up on the rare herbs – even though she had hoped she wouldn't need them. Moving the supplies to the other stretcher was easier and safer for Tony. The more he was jostled, the faster the venom would spread. As gently as they could, Portamer and Pumbint carried Tony back to the ship with Vedagy running to keep up. Morach and Beeb followed with the supplies while Clombic followed – still on alert.

Limdon had set up a makeshift bed in the conference room because the room shared with Beeb was too cramped for Vedagy to attend to the wound. Portamer and Pumbint carefully transferred Tony to the bed and moved out of the way. Vedagy had gone straight to her room to get some supplies and stopped by the kitchen on the way back for a bowl and water.

"Limmy, could you dip this cloth in water and squeeze out the excess, then put it on Tony's forehead? It will at least make him feel a little better. Portamer, could you get me some ice, please? I didn't have enough arms to carry everything when I gathered supplies.

"Tony, can you hear me? How are feeling, honey?"

"It hurts and my leg is tingling," he moaned.

"It will be okay, Tony. You just lie there and rest and we'll get you all fixed up." Vedagy removed Tony's com link so he would be more comfortable, and used the pillow she had brought to elevate his leg higher than his heart. She let the others know to use the telepathy coms unit when they were in the room with Tony, so they didn't worry him. He didn't need that on top of the injury.

*Is it serious? Will he be okay?* Beeb asked.

*It isn't good, but I will do everything I can to make him better. I will need some help for the next little bit. Thank you for the ice, Portamer,* Vedagy acknowledged as he handed her a bowl. They watched as she wrapped some ice in a cloth and held it to the wounded area. *I need to go into the kitchen to boil some herbs for a more effective remedy. Will someone keep the ice on his leg for ten minutes then remove it for ten minutes?*

*I will do it,* Pumbint said.

*Shouldn't you be working on the computer systems?* Portamer asked.

*We may need to move closer to the village so I*

*can get more herbs,* Vedagy added.

*The system is doing a self-diagnostics routine and there is nothing for me to do. It will be done in about four hours. It's much sooner than I expected. I will stay with Tony. You go do what you need to do,* Pumbint insisted.

*Okay. If anything changes, please call me. Remember, another seven minutes on then ten minutes off and repeat ten on. It will slow the venom. Limmy, keep his head cool. Thank you both. I'll be in the kitchen.* With those last instructions, Vedagy ran off to the kitchen with some of the supplies she had collected from her room.

While she was boiling the crown flower in one pan, she began mixing the sesame oil and turmeric in another. When the akra juice was ready, she poured it into the oil mixture and boiled the new concoction together. Though she was tired from the journey to and from the village, her adrenaline had taken over out of concern for Tony. His life was in danger and she was the only one who could help him.

Beeb came into the kitchen with a mournful expression.

"Has something happened, Beeb?" Vedagy asked anxiously.

"Nothing has changed, Veda. Is there an-

ything I can do to help? Tony is the first real friend I've had."

Vedagy wrapped her arms around Beeb and held him for a moment. "The best thing you could do right now is go get some rest." Beeb started to protest, so Vedagy added, "Tony will need your energy when he gets better and you don't want to let him down, right?"

Beeb nodded and started to turn toward his room. "Please let me know when he gets better, Veda. Thank you for helping him."

She wore a sad smile as she watched him slowly walk to his room with his head hung in worry for his friend. Turning back to the stove, she removed the boiling oil and poured it into a cool metal bowl sitting in another bowl of ice. She needed it to cool to room temperature quickly.

When she returned to Tony's side, Limdon was ready to refresh the bowl of water she had been using for Tony's forehead. He was beginning to sweat and his muscles were starting to twitch. Vedagy thanked Pumbint and traded places with him. She applied the gelled oil to the wound and applied a bandage. She then took another bowl of herbs she had mixed with oil and applied it to Tony's forehead. Limdon returned with the water and Vedagy dipped the cloth, and then placed it over the mixture she had just applied.

*Veda, I brought a few crystals and stones with me. They will draw out the poison and help him heal.*

*Thank you, Limmy. Everything will help.*

Vedagy stepped back to allow Limdon to place the crystals around Tony's bed and wound. She used clear quartz around him to aid in general healing and to comfort him. Then she placed bright red-orange rocks called sunstones in a circle around the site of the sting to draw out the poison.

*Now all we can do is wait,* Limdon said as she sat in a chair on the other side of Tony's bed. *Why don't you go get some rest, Veda? You look exhausted.*

*I don't want to leave him. What if he wakes up or gets worse?*

*I will wake you if there is any change. Is there anything I need to do?*

*His wound needs to be cleaned again in one hour and oil reapplied. I will replace the herbs on his forehead now, and they can remain for a while,* she said as she cleaned off the first application of herbs and replaced them with fresh. Taking a cool damp cloth, she placed it over his forehead to keep the herbs moist.

*Let me know right away if his breathing changes. You can moisten his lips with a few drops of water to keep him hydrated, but don't try to get him to drink or eat in case there is swelling inside. I don't know... I need to stay with him.*

*No, you need to get some rest or you won't be any good to him when he does wake.*

*Okay, thank you.* Vedagy looked back at Tony with worry and concern as she left the room.

\* \* \* \* \*

"Sir, the systems are fully functional again."

"Thank you, Pumbint. Have you heard how Tony is doing?"

"Limmy just told me he is waking and Veda is on her way to him. I was just about to go see him myself."

"Very good. I will come with you." Reyclebin and Pumbint met Beeb and Morach as they reached the room. Tony was indeed awake and asking for food. He was back to his old self.

"Did I miss dinner?" Tony asked.

"Tony, you missed three dinners, two breakfasts and two lunches," Beeb told him amidst the laughter.

"No wonder I'm hungry!" Tony said. "What happened? Why is everyone in here and what am I doing in the common room?"

"We'll answer all of your questions in a few minutes, Tony, but first I need to check your wound. I'm so happy you are awake," Vedagy said as she proceeded to check his ankle. The site was completely healed with no signs of infection. The herbs and crystals did their jobs.

"I know you are hungry, Tony, but you need to have broth first because your body needs to get used to eating again. If you do well with the broth, I'll make you some jello and you can have some apple juice. But only if you stay in bed for another day or two to get your strength back."

"Okay, Veda. I'd rather have pancakes, but I did feel a little dizzy when I sat up quickly," Tony dejectedly admitted. Morach and Beeb began to tell Tony all that had tran-spired after he was stung. They were chatting away, so everyone else slipped out of the room.

Per their agreement in a meeting the previous day, Pader set about preparing to take off. They were moving further north to see if they could find Santa. Maybe he could convince the committee that this world was worth saving.

# Profile – Tony

Name:  Tony (toh-nee)
Nickname:  Tony
Planet:  Earth (erth)
Galaxy:  Milky Way (mil-kee way)
Specialty:  Earth knowledge
Dietary Needs:  no restrictions
Other:

> » Orphan – parents recently killed in automobile accident
> » Presumed dead by any who may have looked for him
> » Aspires to be Santa's elf
> » Full of Earth knowledge to help the committee

# Beeb's Fifth Report

Galactic Day 5 –

*I will start where I left off…*

*We were in Hollywood preparing for our next location when Limdon's crystal dislodged from her coms unit while in the hotel. Frinkle saved the day and let her use his to get to the ship because he can pass as human without one.*

*Mr. President chose Uruguay in South America for our next point of interest and we left the United States of America at T minus 504 hours. We landed in a large field with cows in it and made our way to the town – where we were welcomed into the home of one of the local families for a meal. The family was larger than our group and were very happy just enjoying a normal day. When we left them, we went to a place called a bazaar where a group of vendors sell their wares out of doors.*

*A thief tried to steal Clombic's coms unit, but the vendors banded together to protect her. One bad human showed that many others were willing to do a good deed. We left there quickly and departed for another country across the ocean.*

*The navigation system had a malfunction. We landed in the middle of a desert so Pumbint could fix it. While we were there, Vedagy, Clombic, Morach, Tony (the human boy), and I walked to a nearby village for supplies and information. We learned we were in South Africa in the Kalihari desert and Santa Claus (called Father Christmas there) was not due to visit for another two and one-half galactic days.*

*On the way back from the village, Tony was stung by a piscone (known as a scorpion on Earth). Vedagy used her herbs and Limdon used her crystals to heal him, but he was unconscious for two Earth days. Everyone, including me, is thankful he is fully recovered.*

*All computer systems and communications systems are functioning at peak performance. The extra time in the desert also allowed the crystals to recharge to their full capacity. We have ample energy to complete our mission and return home – even if we couldn't continue to recharge them...which we can and will.*

*Everybody is in good health and well rested.*

We are moving to the north and I will report tomorrow. We will be moving quickly to gather more data because of the delays today. We have only one more day before we must return. Maybe if we find Santa Claus, he can answer many of our questions.

This concludes my report for galactic day five on the S.H.A.D.E. mission.

Name: Clombic (cloh-mick)
Nickname: Cloe
Planet: Shascan (shaz-can)
Galaxy: Sherzey (shur-zee)
Specialty: Weapons & combat Expert
Dietary Needs: Carnivore
Other:

   » Sharp-shooter
   » Can build a weapon out of any-thing
   » Women's rights activist
   » Southern accent
   » Protector and bodyguard to the committee

thirteen

## Ethiopia

"Sir, I was going to get a drink of water and discovered we have only one vilkin left," Portamer announced.

"I knew there was something I forgot," Morach said. "We were going to go back to the village to refill the rest of them, but got distracted with Tony's illness and the computer situation. I am sorry, Mr. President."

"Call me Rey...both of you."

"Yes, Sir," they said in unison.

With a slight shake of his head, Reyclebin addressed the water situation. "Pader?"

"Yes, Rey?"

"When you see another area of water, please land so we may fill the vilkin."

"I will at once, Sir. There is a body of water coming up. It appears to be a small stream."

"Wonderful. Set us down as close as you can without notice," Reyclebin instructed.

"Employing the reflector shields and setting down in five minutes. Everyone please prepare for landing," Pader announced the last through the overhead speaker system so all could get buckled into their seats for the landing.

\* \* \* \* \*

"The water supply is just beyond those bushes. I didn't see anyone around it, but I couldn't get a good look in the brush on the other side. I really don't expect any difficulties, but I will take a bow. If necessary, it will look like we are hunting," Clombic announced. She had gone to scout the area briefly.

Again, Vedagy was in the excursion party so she could test that the water was safe to drink. Portamer elected to go this time. He was tired of staying behind and wanted a better look at the area. Limdon said she saw something shimmer as they were landing and wanted to investigate. Besides, she wanted to stretch her legs a little. Morach again joined the party to aid in carrying the vilken.

"Can I go, too?" Tony asked.

"Not this time, Tony. You are still recovering your strength from the scorpion sting," Vedagy said gently.

"But Rey gave me those boots that will protect me..." he tried to argue but was interrupted by Reyclebin.

"I'm sorry, Tony. It is not wise for you to go at this time. There will be other opportunities." Seeing the sad look in Tony's eyes and hoping he wouldn't regret it, Reyclebin added, "perhaps if you, Frinkle, and Beeb can stay within the confines of the awning, you can sit outside to get some fresh air." Tony, Beeb and Frinkle looked at each other and smiled.

The team gathered the vilken and were on their way. Twenty minutes later, they reached the water supply. It was an underground spring that flowed into a pool before making its way down a small stream. The stream was about three feet wide but only one foot deep. Vedagy knelt by the spring, cupped her hand, and scooped up some water. She sniffed it first. It had a strange odor. *Is it sulfur? Maybe it's the smell of the earth and sand.* She wasn't sure what it was but knew it wasn't good for drinking. Out of the corner of her eye, she spotted a boy dressed in only a loin cloth. He had been doing his business in the bushes by the pool of water. She now knew why the water was foul. It was contaminated by human waste.

Several things happened at once. Vedagy told the group not to drink the water, a small group of natives came out of the bushes to gather around the boy, Clombic straightened to her full height and put her hand on her hunting knife, and Limdon spotted the sparkle she had seen from the ship before landing.

Clombic spoke first, addressing the natives, "Hello. We were hunting and needed to fill our water vessels. We mean no harm."

The natives said they were also hunting and came to get water, but they had been told the water here was not good to drink. "There is a place three miles downstream that is safe," a man said. He appeared to be the leader of their small hunting party. Their party was made up of three men and two boys. The boys looked to be in their mid-teens.

Limdon spoke to Vedagy through her coms unit. *Veda, if what I am seeing is real, we may have a way to purify this water.*

*What is it Limmy? Why aren't you saying*

*this to the group?*

*I want to make sure it is what I think it is before getting their hopes up. Can you stall them while I test my theory?*

*Sure. I will let Cloe know. They seem to be talking about hunting techniques right now.*

*Thanks. I'll be right back.* Limdon disappeared to the other side of the pool and through the reeds that grew along the bank.

Vedagy didn't need to stall anyone because their attention was on Clombic and Portamer. Clombic noticed the only things they had to hunt with were their spears and hunting knives. She was telling them they could get better distance with a bow and arrow and would have surprise on their side – because they could hide in the brush while they shot the arrows.

She demonstrated with her bow and proceeded to show them how to use it. She then showed them how they could make their own by using tree limbs and weaving reeds to make a string for the bow. They already knew how to make spears – and arrows are just miniature spears. The natives were busy trying out their new bows and found they worked well.

Portamer was listening intently because

anthropology was the field he taught as a professor. Having contact with natives as primitive as these was exciting for him. Although he didn't show emotion, Vedagy could tell he was in his element. For the first time since they arrived, he was happy he came on this expedition.

Morach had set the vilken on the ground a safe distance from the water while waiting for the water to be tested. He saw Limdon go to the other side of the pool and decided to follow her to lend protection if necessary. He followed her trail through the reeds and stopped suddenly.

There in front of him was Limdon, kneeling on the ground with a reverent look on her face. She was… petting?... a bed of clear rocks. *Those look like the rocks they put around Tony when he was sick. What is she doing? She looks completely in awe.* Clearing his throat, he got Limdon's attention. "Excuse me, Lim, you shouldn't wander off by yourself."

"Hi, Mark. Do you see this?" Her eyes held such wonder and excitement that Morach was taken aback. "It's okay. I have *not* lost my mind," she laughed. "I just haven't seen so much crystal in one place. I am surprised it is here and someone hasn't taken it."

"So, what is it and why is it important?"

"That may have just answered my question of why nobody has taken it," she said with a smile. "This is clear, quartz crystal. From what I've researched, it is found in caves. This is unusual to find a bed out in the open like this." After a moment she looked at Morach and pulled herself together. "Right. It is important, because it can purify the water coming out of the spring. Although the spring water starts out clean, as soon as it touches the contaminated water it becomes contaminated as well. If we could divert the water across this bed of crystals, we could purify the water and make it safe for drinking."

"Well, what are we waiting for? Let's go tell the others," Morach said. He was catching some of her enthusiasm and happy they wouldn't have to go three miles downstream for clean water. They went back to where the group was gathered and Limdon presented her findings and her plan.

The natives liked the idea of not having to go three miles for fresh water. They sent the two boys back to their village, which was about thirty minutes away if they walked. Of course, the boys would probably run and make it there in fifteen minutes. Their mission was to return with the shaman and leader of their tribe, a few more boys and something to dig with.

*Are you there, Rey?* Vedagy called on her coms unit to fill him in on the development.

*Yes, I am here. Is everything okay? Did someone get stung again?*

*Nobody is hurt. Everyone is well. I just wanted to fill you in on what is happening.*

*Good to hear. So tell me what you found,* Rey encouraged, now that he was assured they were safe.

Vedagy proceeded to tell him about the water being contaminated and meeting the hunting party. She also told him about Limdon's plan to redirect the flow from the spring over the quartz bed to purify the water and make it drinkable again. *We will need to wait for the boys to return from the village, so we can dig the new channel, but it won't take long for them to get back. We may be out here for a little while, though.*

*Do you need anything? I could send...*

*I don't think it would be wise to send anyone out here. We wouldn't be able to explain where they came from.*

*Of course. Good thinking. Keep me informed.*

*Thank you, Sir. I made some treats for the boys. They are in the pantry on the second shelf in a square tin. And before you ask, yes. They are for everyone, not just the boys,* Vedagy added with a soft giggle.

Giving a chuckle in return, Reyclebin replied, *Thank you, Veda. I am sure the boys, and the rest of us, will enjoy the treat. We await your safe return.* The connection was closed and Vedagy joined the group once again.

As predicted, the two young men returned quickly with three more young men – and shovel paddles to begin the digging. The shaman, chief, and the chief's wife were coming at a slower pace, but were expected to arrive in the next half hour – at most.

Limdon introduced herself and took one of the shovel paddles. The long-handled shovel was made entirely of wood. The end for digging was elongated, stretching up the handle two feet, forming a paddle one would expect to use for guiding a small boat. Having a wide groove carved down the length of it, the paddle was perfect for digging narrow trenches in the soft dirt and sand. Limdon used the pointed end to scratch a path for the young men to dig.

Before the digging could begin, the   area

needed to be cleared of the brush and reeds. While one young man started on one end and the other at the other end, Limdon showed two more boys the path they needed to dig from the quartz bed back to the stream. There was no sense in creating a whole new stream; they just needed to divert the water to clean it. The water then feeding the stream would not be contaminated and would be safe for everyone along the stream's path. They wouldn't need to travel three miles for fresh water.

The paths were cleared just as the shaman and leader arrived. Morach took over supervising the trench digging.

"This is my father, Chief Ahmed and my mother, Bezawit. Our shaman, Azizama," said Khamel, the first boy they had encountered. Portamer took the lead and introduced himself and the rest of their party.

"I would like to see what you are doing and why," said the shaman. He was skeptical that this outsider knew how to clean the water. He had been blessing it, casting spells on it, and chanting over it ever since people started getting sick from drinking it.

"I found a bed of crystal quartz just on the other side of these reeds. Quartz is a natural purifier, so it can clean the water. We are digging a new path to divert the water from the spring to travel across the quartz and merge back into the natural stream," Limdon explained. "We can then take the dirt we remove from the new channel to create a dam to block off the old path at each end. Eventually, the old water will dry up."

"Why did people start getting sick all of a sudden?" Chief Ahmed asked.

"People are relieving themselves too closely to the water. It then washes into the pond that moves into the stream – and contaminates it," Vedagy explained. "You need to have someone dig a deep hole (away from the water) that your people can use. It will keep the water safer; but it will take time for this area to be cleaned up."

"How long will it take to divert the water; and when can we start using it again?" the shaman asked.

"As soon as the first trench is finished, water will pool over the crystal bed. While the second trench is being dug, we can start to build the dam with reeds and the dirt from the first trench. When both trenches are done and the water starts to be diverted, a dam at the other end will need to be made to keep the bad water from mixing with the good. It will take time to build the dams and for the water to carve the diverted path, but once the water starts running over the crystals, it will be ready for drinking."

Leading the group to the crystal bed and checking the progress of the digging, Limdon showed the chief, shaman, and others what she was talking about.

"We have several of these crystal beds as you call them. They line the stream several times along the way," the shaman said. "We can change the stream so it crosses them to keep the water clean?"

"Yes, you could do that. It will take time and training; but I can teach you, and you can teach the others downstream," Limdon answered. "Cloe, could you show them how to build the dam with reeds and the dirt from the new channel? Don't close it off completely until the first trench is done, though, so we don't flood the area." With a nod, Clombic took two of the young men to teach them how to do the dam. Once they were shown and one of them began on the first dam, she took the other boy to the other end of the pond to get started.

Morach was helping dig the second trench, which was almost completed. He came over to help with the dam – as did the other young man – when the second trench connected to the stream. Clombic went back to the first dam to help. The only thing left was to connect the beginning to the first trench and close up the first dam.

"Ok, this is it. Are we ready?" Limdon asked. Getting a nod of anticipation from everyone, Limdon gave the order. "Go ahead and open up the new trench and close up the dam."

The moment was here. The new path was opened and the water started to move along the channel. Limdon led the group along the stream while she smoothed out a spot (or two) that wasn't as deep as the rest. The water moved faster than they did and reached Portamer within seconds. *"It's working,"* Portamer told Limdon over the coms unit. The water had found the returning trench after pooling over the quartz.

*"It is joining with the stream now,"* Morach added. Just then, he saw Limdon and the group come around the bend – following the

first trench. Although it wasn't a long diversion, it took a few minutes to follow the whole path. Everyone was smiling when they saw it was working.

Vedagy rejoined them as everyone gathered at the crystal bed – which had become a makeshift pool with undercurrents. "Ok, let me test this again. It looks clear and feels cool. The sun may warm it up throughout the day, but it won't get too warm." Scooping a handful, she smelled it and smiled. It smelled clean, not foul like before. She took a little in her mouth and swished it around. With a nod, she swallowed and took another drink. "It's clean and safe now," she said with a smile.

The shaman came to kneel beside Vedagy to test the water himself. He came to the same assessment and relayed the information to the chief and his wife. The young men whooped with joy. Amidst the ensuing laughter, Limdon was thanked. "Don't thank me," she said with a blush. "These young men did most of the work and the crystals were already here."

"We would not have known what to do if you had not happened along," the son of the chief replied. "Thank you for showing us how to do this."

"Bezawit, you may return to the camp and let the women know they can come get fresh water," the chief told his wife. She bowed her head in acknowledgement and turned to leave with excitement in her eyes. This would make their people very happy that clean water was near again.

"May we fill our vessels before traveling on?" Vedagy asked.

"Of course!" the shaman and chief said at the same time. The chief continued, "We cannot thank you enough for this knowledge. This is a community water supply, not just one man's. Anyone can fill from this water. We will have one of our people patrol it to make sure it stays clean, but it is for everyone."

"Thank you," Portamer said. "Mark, will you get the vilken so we can fill them and be on our way before it grows dark?"

"Right away," Morach said as he retraced the new stream back to the spring; which was where he had left the vilken upon their arrival.

Vedagy had been surveying the plants and trees while the channels were being dug.

She found a few trees that would help with the problem of the latrines. She approached the shaman and chief and asked if they would follow her for a moment, then led them to a small grove of cedar and eucalyptus trees. "The leaves from these trees will help keep away the infestation of mosquitoes and other insects that can carry disease when you dig your relieving holes. Dig the holes deep, then drop a bushel of these leaves in before using it. You may wish to cover it with something sturdy to keep children from falling in, but I am sure you can take care to make it safe.

"When it is almost full, throw another bushel of these leaves over the top and let it sit for one moon cycle. At the end of the moon cycle, fill the hole with dirt and do not dig there again for twelve moons," Vedagy explained.

The shaman listened intently with a skeptical look at first. By the time Vedagy was done explaining the procedure, he was nodding and smiling. He could work with this and counsel the chiefs of the other camps on how to do this as well. He was thinking that his prayers had been answered by these foreigners. Even though they looked like all other citizens of Ethiopia, they were clearly not from any nearby camps.

With the vilken filled, the training completed, and additional maintenance instructions given, the foreigners were ready to depart.

"Thank you for your help. We shall make sure the other tribes along the stream are educated and kept safe," the chief said. "You are welcome to come back and visit our camp at anytime."

"Thank you," they said in unison.

Morach turned back as the others started back toward the ship. "Perhaps you can help us. We are looking for Santa Claus," he began. "You may call him Father Noel?"

"Yes, we know of whom you speak. He will not be passing through here for another three weeks. I hear he comes from the north, so it takes him a long time to get here," the chief answered.

"Thank you. Maybe we will cross paths with him on our travels north," Morach said as he turned to catch up to the rest of the group. It would be dark soon and they weren't sure what kinds of animals were in the trees that stood beyond the open prairie they were crossing. Even though the reflector shields were engaged, they could see the ship ahead because they knew what to look for.

* * * * *

Tony, Beeb, and Frinkle were sitting outside under the large umbrella, laughing as they ate. Spotting the returning group, they started to run toward them but were called back by an unseen body before they could get very far.

"They will be here soon, boys. Tony is still regaining his strength and should not be running yet," Pumbint admonished. "You know Rey told you to stay here or you would have to come inside."

Heads hung, they returned to their seats. Suddenly, Beeb had an idea and leaned in to whisper to the other boys. Smiles stretched their mouths and excitement filled their eyes. "We are ready to come in now," Tony said as they picked up their dishes and stepped inside. Wondering what they were up to, Pumbint decided to follow them to the kitchen.

When he saw Frinkle cleaning the dishes

and Beeb and Tony pulling things from the pantry, he understood what they were doing. "I will be right here if you need anything. Just be careful, and don't use the knives or the stove without me," Pumbint said as he took a seat at the table. He would have offered to help, except he knew they wanted to surprise the returning party with something to eat. However, they had only twenty minutes, so he did offer his assistance and asked what they planned to make.

They were just finishing up when they heard Reyclebin greeting the weary party. Pumbint hurried out to help carry in the vilken and greet Limdon. He wanted to see for himself that she and the others were safe. Seeing how tired they were, he took as many vilken as he could carry and told them there was a feast awaiting them in the dining area. He quickly stored the vilken and returned to the kitchen to make sure the boys were ready.

When everyone entered the dining area, they were pleasantly surprised. Beeb, Tony, and Frinkle, with some help from Pumbint, had prepared at least one special dish for each person. "Oh, boys!" Vedagy exclaimed with as much excitement as she could muster after the long day they all had. "I appreciate what you've done. This was so thoughtful. Thank you." *I am so glad I don't have to cook tonight. I know everyone is hungry because we missed lunch, but I'm tired, too. I'll have to do something special for the boys tomorrow.*

"I am so hungry right now," Clombic said as she set down her bow and took her place at the table. "Thank you, Tony, Beeb, Frinkle," she said before digging in to her steak.

"Yes. Thank you," Portamer, Morach, and Limdon each added as they took their seats and began to eat.

"Would you like some tea, milk, soda?" Tony asked. Each gave their drink request and the boys rushed off to fill the orders. When the meal was completed, the group met in the conference room to give their official report to Reyclebin. Beeb was also present as he was the official reporter of their mission. Then they secured themselves in their beds so Pader wouldn't have to wake them when he took off for the next point of contact.

## fourteen

## *Paris*

"Can we find a place to land without being detected?" Reyclebin asked Pader.

"There appears to be an old airfield near Paris that we can land on without being seen. We can quickly transform into the double-decker bus and fit right in with Paris transportation."

"Excellent. Let us know when we need to secure our seats for landing."

\* \* \* \* \*

Portamer, true to his need for knowledge, had researched some of the area's feature attractions where people would most likely congregate. Included in the list were the Eiffel Tower, the Louvre museum, Disneyland resort, and the Notre Dame Cathedral. With this information at hand, they began their tour.

The first thing they noticed was how many couples there were. They were huddled with arms linked as they walked down the street or looked up at the Eiffel Tower. There were also single people milling around and in groups as if they were also part of a tour. Most of them wore smiles as they       enjoyed the lights (even though it was daytime) and decorations announcing the Christmas season. Some even began singing Christmas carols and others around them joined.

Disneyland was still open and full of children and adults enjoying the festivities despite the cold weather and approaching holiday. The patrons were enjoying the rides and food, as well as the Disney characters that stopped and signed autographs or posed for pictures. They certainly looked happy.

The committee members decided to find out what all the fuss was about and went on a few rides. Portamer, Frinkle, Beeb, and Tony each had cotton candy in a rainbow of colors. Vedagy had a veggie burger and the others had hotdogs. Vedagy also insisted the boys have a hotdog or hamburger to counteract the sugar. Portamer, of course, had seconds of cotton candy. Being sated and tired from the walking and excitement, they decided to return to the bus.

The sun may have been setting, but the city was anything but dark. Paris was not known as the City of Lights without reason. The normal white lights were complemented with multi-colored lights from Christmas decorations. The team congregated on the top deck of the bus to get a good look at the city lights. They sat in silence enjoying the scenery before turning in for the night. They needed to get up early to observe more people.

In the morning at breakfast, Tony let the group know that he had talked to Santa's helper at Disneyland. "He said the real Santa is in Finland, at his workshop, getting ready for his trip Christmas Eve. That's only two days away."

"Why didn't you tell us earlier?" Morach asked. He had moved to the edge of his seat when Tony began telling them his tale. He was looking forward to seeing Santa again since they parted at Universal Studios in California.

"I'm sorry, Mark. I was having so much fun that I totally forgot. But I did write a letter to him while I was there."

"Really? What did you say?" Beeb asked excitedly.

"I just said we were trying to find him and asked him to meet us in Finland."

"Well, we certainly will go to Finland next as our time is running short," Reyclebin said. "But we still have four days on Earth so I think we should take today to continue our study while we are here."

"That sounds reasonable. After all, our mission is to find happiness on Earth, not just to find Santa Claus," Portamer reminded everyone.

"You are correct, Portamer. Let us finish our meal and we will visit the Louvre and the cathedral today," Reyclebin announced.

Portamer was pleased with the decision. He was interested in seeing the museum for the historical significance. Maybe it held a clue to people's happiness. Tony and Morach were not thrilled with the turn of events, but they had no authority to change the outcome.

This was the city of love, so Pumbint and Limdon wanted to experience some of the lure. Clombic was interested in seeing the weapons even if they were only depicted in sculptures and paintings. She suspected she would find various forms of bows, spears, and knives, but they would still be interesting.

Anticipation was heavy in the air as they drove to The Louvre. Vedagy and Reyclebin stayed behind so Pader could enjoy the museum with everyone else. They were to return for lunch or enjoy one of the many cafés on the grounds.

The building was beautiful and took up several city blocks. It did not disappoint any of them. They even viewed the famous painting of the Mona Lisa before they went separate directions. Portamer and Clombic headed to the history section, Pumbint and Limdon headed to the Greek sculptures of the Gods, while the rest decided to join a group touring the paintings.

When it came time for lunch, Pumbint and Limdon found a romantic bistro that several other couples had already found. There were only a few tables for two available outside the café. They found one in the center, allowing them seclusion amongst others. Anyone could see they were in love and fit right in with the other lovers partaking of the atmosphere and food.

Portamer and Clombic rejoined the rest of the group, minus Pumbint and Limdon, and found a fast-food place that had something for everyone. They decided to get some extra to take back to Vedagy and Reyclebin on the bus. It wasn't fair that Vedagy had to cook for everyone all the time. Even though some of them helped her on occasion, she did the majority of the work. She was their own mother hen and they all appreciated her.

Reyclebin and Vedagy had just finished eating when Pumbint and Limdon returned. Everyone gathered in the conference room on the second level of the bus while Pader drove them to the Notre Dame cathedral.

"We heard people talking happily as they confessed their love," Pumbint said as he gazed lovingly at Limdon. "We even saw a man propose marriage to a woman in the middle of the courtyard," Limdon added.

"Is that what that man was doing on his knee in front of the glass structure?" Vedagy asked. At their nods, she continued with her hands clasped to her chest. "Aww. That is so romantic."

"What did you find, Portamer?" Reyclebin asked.

"Clombic and I went to the historical exhibits and were intrigued by them. Did you know that humans evolved from amphibians?"

"Excuse me, Portamer," Reyclebin interrupted, "I was referring to the happiness mission."

"Of course, Sir. We saw several groups of people who were in awe of the displays and historical information. While that may be, we couldn't discern happiness over interest."

"That was my conclusion, also," Clombic replied to Portamer's look for additional information.

Reyclebin looked to Morach who was the eldest in the final group. "We think there is sufficient evidence of happiness, so we see it everywhere," Morach confessed. Beeb, Frinkle, and Tony snickered as they agreed with Morach.

"I would like a less biased report when you return from the cathedral," Reyclebin admonished. "I know you are anxious to meet Santa, but he isn't the only source we need. In order to convince the Galactic Council not to destroy Earth, we need to have more evidence."

Morach and the boys, sufficiently chastised, murmured their acknowledgement.

"I would like to go to the cathedral," Vedagy requested.

"Ok, anyone else have a preference?"

"I would like to stay here this time," Tony and Morach said together.

"The rest of you will be going, then," Reyclebin said.

So it was that Pader, Portamer, Pumbint, Beeb, Limdon, and Clombic went as a group to tour Notre Dame. Hundreds of people toured the cathedral daily. Only twenty people were allowed to begin the tour each hour, so they were in a group with fourteen other people... nine of which were children.

There wasn't a lot of time for conversation during the tour as they learned the history of Notre Dame. The cathedral was built over 850 years ago and went through several renovations – including the replacement of the massive organ and the famous bells. Walt Disney's movie 'The Hunchback of Notre Dame' immortalized the cathedral for generations to come. The children started chattering that they had seen the movie, but were quickly told to quiet down as the tour continued.

The committee returned to the bus when the tour was completed; but, although they enjoyed the excursion, they didn't have any new information regarding happiness. Reyclebin gave in and directed Pader to set a new course for Lapland, Finland. Hopefully, this Santa Claus would give them enough information to save Earth.

# *Profile – Portamer*

Name: Portamer (por-tuh-mer)
Nickname: Portamer
Planet: Dunkis (dun-kiss)
Galaxy: Trimusk (try-musk)
Specialty: Professor of Anthropology
Dietary Needs: Sugar
Other:
  » Comes from a planet of
     skeptics
  » Studied Earth's historical origin
  » Little patience for frivolities

## fifteen

## Meeting Santa

*Dear Santa,*

*You might know that my friends are trying to find happiness on Earth. I told them how you give happiness to everyone, so they want to meet you. But we just miss you every time we get close. We are going to Finland where we heard you have your village. It would be so cool if you could be there and meet my friends. It would really mean a lot to me.*

*Thanks, Tony*

*P.S. If you have an opening in your workshop, I'd really like to be one of your elves.*

"It appears our guests will arrive at any time, Nate. Please meet them at the village and ask that *all* of them follow you…including Rey."

"Certainly, Santa."  Nathaniel motioned for three other elves to join him in the village. Nathaniel found the ship disguised as a bus easily enough, but the hard part was convincing Reyclebin and Pader to accompany them. "Your ship will be fine, Sir.  Santa has requested that everyone, including you and Pader, join him in the workshop. He is getting ready for his midnight deliveries and regrets he couldn't meet you himself."

"How did you know our names and why did you call our bus a ship?" Portamer asked.

"All will be answered when you meet Santa.  Follow me."  Nathaniel led the party (Reyclebin and Pader reluctantly included) through the gift shop, through the petting zoo, and into a cave with a secret entrance at the back.

When they cautiously stepped through the entrance, they stopped and looked around in wonder and awe.  The cave opened up to an amazingly bright and cheerful city.  Elves were everywhere… loading gifts on the sleigh, grooming the reindeer, running back and forth between buildings, and talking to a large man with a white beard and white curly hair that reached his shoulders. He was wearing a white t-shirt, black boots (being polished by another elf), and red velvet pants with white silk cuffs held up with black suspenders adorned with red and white candy canes.

"You must be Santa Claus," Reyclebin said as he extended his hand toward Santa. "I've been told a lot about you by these two." Morach and Tony stood to his left. Their smiles couldn't possibly get any bigger.

"Hi, Santa!" they said in unison.

"Was it really you that helped Mark in California?" Vedagy asked.

"Yes, it was, Veda. I knew you all would be here before you left for your home planets, but I didn't know when until I got Tony's letter. Thank you, Anthony. Because of your letter, I had time to prepare your rooms. Please follow Nate to the lodge. He will show you to your rooms."

"But..." Tony stopped when Santa held up his hand.

"You get settled into your room while I finish up some preparations and I will meet you for dinner in an hour. Okay?" Santa got a nod and a smile from all of them as they turned to follow Nate to the lodge.

"He sure is friendly and hospitable," Clombic said. She was impressed to find that a bar had been hung for her to sleep on – or rather, hang from.

"Oh," Nate added, "I almost forgot. Santa said you may come to dinner in your true forms without fear. He can see them anyway, so there is no reason not to be comfortable." With that announcement, Nate left them to help Santa complete his final preparations.

"Wow! Did you see your room? Come look at mine! It looks like New York!" Frink told Beeb and Tony excitedly. "There's even clothes for me! Did you have clothes in your room, too?"

"I haven't looked in the closet yet, but I love it – everything is Christmas! That's my favorite thing in the whole world!" Tony answered with his own burst of energy. "What does yours look like, Beeb?"

"Mine has stars everywhere – the ceiling, the floor, the walls, the bed, the closet, every-where!" In addition to his tone, the other two could tell he was excited by the way his eyes lit up. "And my closet has star clothes so I can be myself! I don't have to hide as a human here." Realizing what he just said, he apologized. "Uh, sorry, Tony. I didn't mean anything by that."

"No problem, Beeb. It's not your fault I'm human!" They started laughing again and went to visit each other's rooms; then went back to their own to change for dinner. The others were changing in their rooms as well. Nate came to collect them exactly one hour after he had left them and led them to the dining hall.

"Welcome!" Santa said with a smile when they came into the room. "Please take your seats."

Again they were amazed at the accommodations to their diets as well as their seating needs: Vedagy had a booster seat; Reyclebin had a wide chair that looked like a large, three-sided box to help him keep from flattening into a puddle from the gravity; Clombic had a low stool; Beeb had a wide, high-backed, waterproof chair; and the rest had regular human dining chairs with high backs. They took their seats and looked toward the head of the table where Santa sat.

"Let me introduce my lovely wife, Mrs. Claus." Santa swept his hand toward the other end of the table where his wife sat.

"Please call me Gerty. It's short for Gertrude." Still smiling, Mrs. Claus welcomed them to their home. "We are very pleased you came to meet us. It isn't often we receive a visit from such distinguished guests as your-selves. I certainly hope you enjoy your stay with us."

When the meal was nearing an end, Santa announced, "I have a surprise for Morach, Tony, and Portamer. I would like you three to join me on my trip tonight. Now, before you refuse, Portamer, it will give you some addi-tional insight to happiness." Frinkle looked at the three with envy before he congratulated them. "Don't worry, Frinkle, you will have your turn to ride in my sleigh before you go home," he added with a wink. Just then, Frinkle knew that Santa knew his secret and winked back at him.

"Why did you choose me?" Portamer asked. He couldn't imagine why he was chosen over Beeb or Frinkle. Or even Vedagy, for that matter. *Santa must have some reason. I will have to pay close attention.*

"I believe you will discover the answers you seek tonight," he replied with his signature smile. His lips were turned upward exposing perfectly white teeth and pushing his pink, round cheeks so high his twinkling eyes narrowed. "I don't have room for everyone tonight, but I can give you a brief ride tomorrow evening if you like.

"This evening, however, I would like you to feel comfortable. I know you have been confined to the ship for most of your time on Earth, Reyclebin. Please take time to stroll through the village. The dome over our hidden city may look like a mountain of ice from the outside, but it is climate controlled on the inside and you need not fear freezing or melting."

Santa rose from his chair as Nathaniel entered the room, tapping the face of his wristwatch with his fingernail. He silently sent a message with his raised eyebrows and pursed lips – signaling the time to go was fast approaching if Santa was to keep on schedule. Clearing his throat, Santa told the three passengers to quickly change into the special clothes laid out for them in their rooms and to meet him outside in fifteen minutes. To the others, he bid a good night, promising to see them at lunch tomorrow.

## *Profile – Santa*

Name:

» Santa Claus; Kris Kringle; Papa Noel; Father Christmas; St. Nicholas

Address:

» Lapland, Finland (near polar ice cap – recently moved from North Pole, Alaska)

Occupation:

» Spread happiness around the world and deliver gifts to good boys and girls sixteen

## *Christmas*

The three chosen passengers, dressed in their specified outfits, took their places in the sleigh. Santa called out to the eight reindeer, harnessed to the front, to begin their flight. Tony, looking at home in his deep green outfit, joined in calling out the reindeer names with delight.

Portamer had never ridden in a vehicle that allowed the wind to whoosh over and around him, causing his ears to ring. It's a good thing Santa gave him specially made goggles that fit over his three-lens glasses so his eyes wouldn't burn and dry out.

He had opted to wear the suit he was issued at the beginning of the mission under the outfit Santa gave him. He was more than a little concerned that he would be too cold with the weather and the open conveyance. However, he was now rethinking the wisdom of that decision.  Maybe he should learn to trust more.

The Earth clothing, snug yet allowing ample room for movement, was protecting against the elements rather nicely.  He made quite the sight adorned in a purple pair of velvety pants and a purple jacket with golden fur lining the bottom edge, the cuffs of the sleeves, and the edge of the hood that had slipped off his head.  The big purple buttons stood out against the golden fur-lined edge of the jacket, forming a line down the length of the jacket right in the middle of his body. Completing the ensemble was a polished pair of deep  purple, almost black, boots with golden fur around the top to keep his feet dry from the snow and rain.  His pants were tucked into the top of the boots.

He was quite pleased with the royal purple and the golden fur that brought out the gold flecks in his deep purple eyes, and honored to have a suit just like Santa's but in a different color. Santa's suit, of course, was red and white with black buttons. Yes, Portamer could see how Santa was perceived as one who spreads happiness.

"Is that the White House?" Tony

exclaimed as they flew around, not over, the American President's home.

"Yes it is, Tony." Santa explained that they couldn't fly directly over the White House because it was considered a 'no-fly zone', which meant nobody could pass through the zone unless they wanted to be shot down. He didn't think that would be a wise thing to do considering he had a lot of homes to visit.

"How do you deliver presents if you can't fly over it?" Morach inquired. He was leaning over the edge of the sleigh to see the wondrous grounds. Fortunately, he was seat-belted in so he couldn't fall out. Just the same, Santa cautioned him and he pulled back inside a bit. It was amazing seeing the Earth's vegetation from a different vantage point. Everything looked so small yet so vast at the same time.

"This is one of those times I have to rely on some help from my friends on the ground. I have a special pass that allows me to enter the grounds, with the reindeer and sleigh, so that I can deliver the gifts. After all, even the President's children deserve to have gifts from Santa, too."

After delivering presents to the White House and to all the other children, it was time to return to Santa's secret village. The sun was just starting to rise as they were flying over Russia. Morach and Tony had fallen asleep somewhere over Asia. Portamer was still hanging on by a thread, but was awake enough to enjoy the rising sun's golden rays creeping along the horizon and filling the land with light. If he were honest with himself, he would admit that he had enjoyed the excursion. A slight smile was on his face when Santa turned to him.

"Did you enjoy yourself, Portamer?" he asked.

"As a matter of fact, it was enlightening to see the way in which you deliver happiness. You do this only one time per year?"

"Actually, different countries celebrate at different times; which actually makes my job easier. Some celebrate early on December sixth while most countries celebrate on December 25th and some don't celebrate until January 5th. Yes, I have to make three trips, but it's more manageable than trying to deliver to the whole world in one night."

"That makes sense and explains why we

passed over large areas. I recall when we were in Ethiopia that they said you wouldn't be coming for a few more weeks. Now I understand."

"We will be landing soon. Maybe we should wake these two," Santa said as he gently shook Tony's shoulder. Portamer tried to rouse Morach, but both were unsuccessful. They decided to let them sleep. The boys looked content – smiling as they slumbered. It was easy to tell they had enjoyed their trip.

After landing successfully, Santa said, "The elves will return the reindeer to their stalls, brush them, and feed them. They did most of the work tonight and will probably sleep for a week to rest up for the next trip." Looking at Tony and Morach, he added, "We can carry these two to their beds or we can let them sleep in the sleigh. They will probably enjoy waking in the sleigh later."

"Yes, they probably would. I am not sure I can carry myself, let alone a sleeping boy," Portamer replied. With an acknowledging chuckle, they decided to let the sleeping boys lie. They retired to their rooms after Santa told Portamer to sleep as long as he liked. Christmas dinner would be around six o'clock, which was almost twelve hours away.

\* \* \* \* \*

While Santa and his helpers got some much needed rest, Vedagy and the others helped Mrs. Claus make the Christmas feast: a beautiful, golden-brown turkey with corn-bread stuffing and cranberry chutney; honey-baked ham; buttery, smooth, mashed potatoes; succulent candied yams; crunchy, glazed carrots; fruity ambrosia salad; and homemade, fluffy, light-bread biscuits. In addition, they made creamy fudge, creamy pumpkin pies, sweet pecan pies, fluffy divinity candy and sugar cookies. They had just finished decorating the last of the sugar cookies when Tony and Morach came in with tousled hair, still wearing their suits from the previous night.

With a smile and barely suppressed chuckle, Mrs. Claus held open her arms for them to come forward and wrapped them each in a warm, motherly hug. "I think you should probably take a shower and get changed for dinner," she said as she led them to the wing housing their rooms.

On their way, Tony came fully awake and

he remembered the night before. Turning to Mrs. Claus and walking backwards, his excitement bubbled over and his words tripped over each other. "Oh, Mrs. Claus, it was great! We rode in the sleigh and visited the White House – we didn't go in, but we were there – and we flew over the ocean! Oh, oh, oh, and I got to call out the reindeer names when we took off! And, best of all, we got to sleep in the sleigh!" His eyes were sparkling with so much joy that it was contagious.

Morach added his bit. Mrs. Claus smiled and chuckled at such a show of exuberance. Both continued to chatter as they made their way to their rooms. Arriving, Mrs. Claus ushered each to his room and urged them both to hurry back. She heard Portamer exiting his room and offered to walk back to the dining room with him.

"Did you enjoy yourself last evening, Portamer?"

"It was very enlightening. We were able to observe a few children opening their gifts and the faces of the parents were filled with such joy and love – just from watching the excited actions of their children."

"Yes, it is more powerful and fulfilling to

give than to receive. You may be convinced, after all, that happiness does exist on Earth," Santa added as he joined the two. He pulled Mrs. Claus into a quick hug and gave her a peck on the cheek before continuing on with them.

The elves were gathered in the banquet room and applauded as Santa entered the room. "Congratulations on another successful delivery, Santa," Nathaniel said as he held up a glass of punch.

"It wasn't just me, I had help last night," he pointed out. "Tony, where are you?" Santa asked as he looked around the room. Not seeing him, he asked for Morach. Just as Mrs. Claus started whispering in his ear that the two were changing clothes, they came skidding into the room. "Here they are." Santa put an arm around each one and squeezed Portamer's shoulder as he came up beside Tony. "These fine gentlemen were my assistants last night. They deserve credit for a successful trip as well." Santa beamed proudly as cheers went up from everyone in the room. "Let's eat!" he proclaimed.

Santa carved the turkey as a line formed along the buffet tables. This system was much easier and quicker than passing hot dishes around the room. Laughter and praise for the delectable food was heard throughout the room as everyone enjoyed the meal.

*Profile – Presents*

Purpose:
» Share happiness with others and let them know they are special

Types of Presents:
» Gifts may be tangible (store bought or handmade) or may be intangible (sharing a meal, a smile, quality time)

<u>WARNING!</u>
» Giving presents can be extremely fulfilling! Use caution when delivering gift and be prepared for a big smile in return.
» Although, it is also very nice to receive a gift in return, it is in the giving that is the true reward.

## seventeen

# Gifts

After dinner was done and the leftovers were put away, Mrs. Claus nodded to Vedagy and Frinkle. They went to the cupboards to retrieve the gifts they had hidden there. Vedagy handed out her gifts. Clombic opened hers first and found a beautiful dress tailored to fit her. "How? Where? When?" she started in surprise. "Thank you, Veda. It's beautiful!"

"I got it in Uruguay and altered it while you were digging ditches in Ethiopia," she replied happily. "Limmy, this gift is for you."

"Oh, Veda! It is beautiful! And pink! My favorite color! Thank you!" Limdon beamed when she saw the dress Vedagy had altered for her.

Frinkle, Tony, and Beeb were next. They each received a pair of special socks to keep their feet dry and warm. Pumbint received a jar of oil made from herbs to keep his tools from rusting. Reyclebin received some herbal tea to help him sleep and Pader received an herbal tea to keep him awake while he was driving or flying. "Portamer, I found this in Uruguay and thought it would suit you," Vedagy said as she handed over his gift. Portamer opened the package and found a bright red t-shirt sporting a map of South America, with Uruguay slightly larger than the other countries. Montevideo was identified with an arrow and the words 'You are here'.

Tony looked at it for a second or two then a light bulb must have gone off as his puzzled look changed to one of understanding. "I get it! You are a professor and this shows a map and someplace we visited! You could use this in your classes about your time on Earth."

"I suppose I could, Tony. Thank you, Vedagy. I appreciate your kindness."

"Yes, thank you, Veda," several of the others echoed Portamer's thanks.

Blushing with a smile that lit up her whole face, she replied, "You are all welcome."

Frinkle nudged Beeb and Tony as he stood with a gift in his hands. "Veda, this is from all of us." She smiled at them and opened the small package. It was wrapped in newspaper with a silver ribbon around it.

"Oh, boys, this is beautiful!" She immediately took the seashell encrusted comb and put it in her hair. Though she didn't have much hair, it was enough that she could put the comb through the top of her bangs. "How do I look?" she asked as she turned her head one way then the other to model it.

"Perfect!" "Gorgeous!" "Very pretty!" They all answered at once.

"Thank you. All of you."

"Portamer, I got something for you when we were in South Africa," Morach said as he handed over a heavy package. When Portamer opened it and looked at the relic questioningly, Morach explained. "It's a ceremonial mask used in weddings a hundred years ago."

"I don't know what to say, Morach. It was very thoughtful. Thank you."

"I know what to say," Tony said. "Is that why the stretcher was so heavy?" His voice was full of awe, not anger. Then he laughed and others joined in.

"My gift to each of you is an album of

photographs, so you remember your time here. They will be completed before you leave. That's why you've seen Nathaniel flashing the camera during your stay here," Santa said. Everyone was excited at the prospect of having something to show their friends and family when they returned home.

"And these are my gifts to each of you," Mrs. Claus said as she handed out the soft packages. Each one contained a knit hat, scarf, and gloves and each set was a different color – when they put them on, they looked like a rainbow.

Yawns were discreetly hidden behind hands, and eyelids were starting to droop. It was time for bed. With thanks given again, everyone gathered their gifts and shuffled toward their rooms.

"Portamer, could I have a word with you, please?" Santa asked. Mrs. Claus gave Santa a peck on the cheek and said she would be in their room. "There's one more gift to give." He handed over a small, unwrapped box.

"Santa, thank you. I already have glasses, though. Why would you give me something I already have?" Portamer asked confusedly.

"Ah, Portamer. These are special glasses.

While they are practical in the normal sense, they also allow you to see the truth in everything."

Portamer put them on and finally understood. Nobody had ever given Portamer a gift before tonight. These selfless acts of kindness gave him a feeling he never had before – true happiness. This new sensation brought tears of joy to his three, purple eyes. Portamer was finally a believer! He now knew that happiness existed on Earth. There is also sadness, but there is an overwhelming amount of happiness that is found in many acts: viewing a sunset with someone you love, watching children play, giving to others, receiving from others without expectations of reciprocating, helping someone less fortunate, and many others. Portamer now knew that happiness was different to everyone and each person had a right to pursue that happiness.

"Santa, you must come back to headquarters with us. Our people need you to help spread this joy," Portamer said excitedly.

"Portamer, my friend, you know I cannot do that. I am needed here. But I will tell you something else about those glasses. The left lens allows you to see if someone has been naughty or nice. The right lens lets you see everything you need to know about a person – name, age, address, occupation, etc. But the middle lens is the best. It allows you to know what would make a person happiest," Santa began. "So you see, Portamer, you have the same gift I have. You can go back to your galaxy and do the same job I do. I am the Santa of planet Earth. You are now the Universal Santa – spreading joy and happiness to all the galaxies."

"Really? I wouldn't know what to do or how to do it! Where do I begin?"

"There are some rules, Portamer. First, always keep the location of your workshop a secret. You found mine by sheer determination and some help from me.

"Second, have fun. Do not make it a chore for you or your elves. Spreading joy should not be something you regret. It will take hard work; but it will be work done with a light heart, knowing you are making dreams come true. And the most important rule of all: have someone you trust as your head elf and someone you love as your wife and partner."

"There is someone I have had my eyes on... But about the elf..." he began. His eyes widened in surprise as he suddenly had an idea. "I think I know the perfect person for the job! Do you think he will accept?"

"I am sure Tony would be excited and honored to be your head elf, Portamer. See, you are already making dreams come true!"

# Profile –Truth Glasses

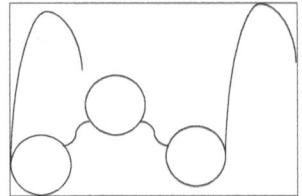

Left lens:

&raquo; Shows if someone has been naughty or nice.

Right lens:

&raquo; Gives personal information: name, address, occupation, how many children in the family and much more.

Middle lens:

&raquo; Shows what would make someone the happiest.

# Beeb's Sixth Report

Galactic Day 6 –

*I am writing this while we are traveling back to Buffinger to report to the Galactic Council.*

*Shortly after we left the desert in South Africa at T-minus 336 hours, Morach discovered we had only one vilkin of water left; so we set down in another part of Africa, called Ethiopia, to refill the vilken. Vedagy and Limdon determined that the water source was not safe for consumption, but Limdon was able to show the natives how to purify the water. We were able to refill the vilken and travelled further north.*

*We landed in Paris, France, and visited several tourist attractions to assess the happiness of the most people we could in the shortest time possible. We saw signs of happiness among the couples in cozy cafés and while wandering around the tourist spots. There was a Santa's helper in the children's theme park and Tony wrote a letter to the real Santa – after finding out his location. We decided that we would go straight there since time was running out.*

*We arrived in Lapland, Finland, and Santa's head elf, Nathaniel, insisted Mr. President and Captain Pader both join Santa with the rest of us. Our ship was hidden and safe.*

*Santa had to deliver gifts soon after we arrived and invited Tony, Morach, and Portamer to accompany him. They witnessed happiness in children receiving gifts and parents giving them. After they returned and rested, we had a really big feast then exchanged gifts that we purchased or made for each other. Mrs. Claus made a hat, scarf, and mittens for each of us. Nathaniel digitized much of our visit and Santa gave us each a portfolio to commemorate our stay.*

*We spent the next 24 hours relaxing, visiting, and comparing observations. We also said our goodbyes to Frinkle. He decided to stay behind with his cousin Frankle. Since he can pass as human, it won't be a problem for him. Frankle said he could get Frinkle a job with Mr. Hardgold, so he would be able to take care of his needs. We were both happy and sad that he decided to stay. Santa promised to give Frinkle a ride back to New York in his sleigh in a few days when he made his next delivery.*

*We have learned that Earth is based on balance. For every action there is a reaction. There is both good and evil, happiness and sadness, giving and receiving, etcetera. It is our consensus that sufficient happiness has been found on Earth and the planet should be preserved.*

*This concludes my final report for the mission to Search for Happiness and Assess the Destiny of Earth.*

## *Galactic-Day to Earth-Hours Conversion Table*

| # of Galactic days | hours @ start of day | hours @ end of day | t-minus (end of day) |
|---|---|---|---|
| 1 | 0 | 168 | 1008 |
| 2 | 168 | 336 | 840 |
| 3 | 336 | 504 | 672 |
| 4 | 504 | 672 | 504 |
| 5 | 672 | 840 | 336 |
| 6 | 840 | 1008 | 168 |
| 7 | 1008 | 1176 | 0 |

# Epilogue

"You have read the reports and heard the testimony. I would like to give you one more point to ponder before we reconvene tonight. I read a sign depicting a quote from a great poet on Earth. It is titled 'Happiness':

> "*The happiness of life is made up of minute fractions – the little, soon-forgotten charities of a kiss, a smile, a kind look, a heartfelt compliment in the disguise of a playful raillery, and the countless other infinitesimals of pleasant thought and feeling.*"
> --Samuel Taylor Coleridge

\* \* \* \* \*

"Has everyone had ample time to ponder the evidence and reach a decision?"

Receiving the expected nods, Reyclebin asked them to use their indicators if they agreed there was sufficient evidence that Earth should continue as it was. All indicators lit up.

"Ok, it is decided. Earth shall *not* be destroyed," Reyclebin, Chairman of the Committee to Search for Happiness and Assess the Destiny of Earth and President of the Universal Council of Galaxies, announced with great satisfaction and relief.

The members of S.H.A.D.E., along with Pader and Tony, cheered loudly. Laughter ensued, and Portamer began thinking of his future as Universal Santa as he reached into his pocket and felt the glasses that would assist him.

--The End--

## About the Author

Ms. Starr has lived in several states and two foreign countries, but always returns to her home state of Oregon.

She currently lives in Springfield, Oregon with two roommates, two cats, and a dog.